EDITORIAL REVIEW

I0593063

Cosy Burrow Books

Thor's Dragon Rider
Book One

SAFEGUARD

"Kara's back for another adventure in Katrina Cope's latest book, *Safeguard*, with Kara's loyal dragon, Elan, and her wingless Valkyrie friends. Just when her new life seems to be drearily peaceful, a terrifying prophecy about Loki's illegitimate children threatens to destroy Asgard's hard-won tranquility." Amanda K., Line Editor, Red Adept Editing

NORSE DRAGON BOOKS

Valkyrie Academy Dragon Alliance

Series

Marked Prequel

Chosen

Vanished

Scorned

Inflicted

Empowered

Ambushed

Warned

Abducted

Besieged

Deceived

Thor's Dragon Rider Series

Safeguard

Pursuit

Entrapment

Safeguard

Ebook first published in USA in August 2020 by Cosy Burrow
Books

Ebook first published in Great Britain in August 2020 by Cosy
Burrow Books

www.katrinacopebooks.com

Text Copyright © 2020 by Katrina Cope

Cover Design Copyright © art4artists.com.au

Published by Cosy Burrow Books

All rights reserved

ISBN: 9780648766179

To the lovers of dragons - your next dragon friend awaits within these pages.

Chapter One

"**B**attle Maiden! Get me another mead!"

I glare at the bushy-haired redhead raising his pewter cup. Remnants from his last mead dribble down his wild auburn beard.

He smiles, showing off his straight teeth. "Please," he says smartly, as though it were an afterthought. His smile broadens. The warrior's muscles along his thick arm ripple as he pushes the cup forward, holding it high.

With my hands by my side, I flick each finger, one by one, and shake my head in disbelief. Sometimes it takes all of my effort not to clop the god of thunder over the head. If he weren't so lovable, by gods and myself alike, I probably would have pressured Odin for a different position. Scattered food and empty plates cover the table, proving hard to avoid as I lean over the mess to grab the tankard out of his hand. I prop a hand on my hip while still leaning over his mess. "Thor, you know I don't like being called that."

He smacks me on the arm as a friendly gesture, and my thin form lurches to the side from the force. "I know that. I was just making sure you didn't miss my father. I'm sure you miss Odin bossing you around and not calling you by your name." He winks.

A strand of my long dark hair falls over my face, and I hook it behind my ear. "Ah, actually. I don't miss him and the way he used to rule the Valkyries, but you know, even he calls me by my name now."

Thor grabs my cheek and shakes it. "Ah, Kara. I know the name to your pretty little face. I'm just messing with you. Now, be a dear and get me that mead."

With a numb cheek from Thor's grasp, I walk through the ruckus of the hall. Merriment surrounds me as warriors dine and celebrate. Serious battles have been rare lately. They've had ample time to fill between practices, and celebrate they do. The Valhalla warriors pack these hours with gaiety and celebration that impress the gods immensely, several of whom have joined them.

The large bowl containing mead lies outside the hall under some branches of Yggdrasil at the far end of the celebration. Of course, the world tree with the never-ending pot of mead is on the opposite end of Valhalla. I sigh and weave through the crowd, proving my hours of sparring and training were useful—at least to dodge rowdy warriors. It's a tight fit through the hall crammed with einherjar, making me glad I'm wearing my black fighting leathers instead of a dress. It wasn't a hard choice, seeing as someone has to work and keep an eye on Thor when he's celebrating.

A warrior crashes into me from behind, shoving me forward and straight into a wall of fur. I push against the coarse fibers and crane my neck to stare into the deep-brown eyes of a large hound at least a head taller than the majority of the warriors here.

A deep growl rumbles in the hound's throat. "Watch it!" The hound pulls back his lips, showing off his long canines.

I blink in disbelief. "Sorry, Fenrir." I'm used to the hound speaking our language, but usually, he's an adorable pup.

"Stop it, Fenrir. Kara is a friend. You know that." Tyr pushes his bulky form past Fenrir and stands between us, making my average height feel small against the tall god and massive hound. Tyr scratches his trimmed beard, and his brown eyes gaze at me apologetically. "I'm sorry. I don't know what's gotten into him lately."

Fenrir snorts at the back of the god of justice's head, blowing Tyr's long dark hair over his face.

I got to know this large hound over the last couple of years. Reminding myself that he is usually an adorable pup, I slowly raise a hand to Fenrir's crest. My Caucasian skin tone looks paler against his dark fur as I rub him. I add a special sweetness to my voice, trying to calm the oversized hound. "Oh, Fenrir. Are you feeling unwell?"

Fenrir growls, exposing his large canines again, and I hastily retract my hand.

"Come, Fenrir. Let's get you out of here." The muscles in Tyr's arms bulge as he coaxes the hound away from the crowd.

I watch Tyr and Fenrir retreat, the god's hand resting comfortingly on the hound's shoulders as they exit. The god of war and justice took a liking to the large hound when he was a pup and continued to raise him when the other gods were intimidated by his size.

A drunken warrior stumbles and collides with me, the pewter cup in my hand clashing with his. The noise reminds me of my task, and I continue to the large pot of mead, dipping the mug into the barrel.

A large goat's head pokes out of the leaves, startling me by the sudden appearance of horns and eyes.

I throw my hand over my heart. "Oh, Heidrun! You made me jump."

The goat bleats, and I scratch it around the ear, burying my fingertips in the brown fur before picking a few leaves from Yggdrasil and feeding them to the goat.

"Eat up, special goat. You have a lot of thirsty warriors to keep happy."

I saw goats on Midgard and was surprised to discover that they produced milk, not mead. It was then that I learned that Heidrun is one of a kind. If her food source consists only of foliage from the world tree, then she will continue to supply mead for the warriors of Valhalla.

With Thor's flask full of mead, I weave through the crowd and return to the burly redhead.

"Oh. Thank you, dear," Thor booms, grabbing the cup from me. He sees my face and chuckles. "Kara. You know I like you."

My mouth quirks to the side, unimpressed. "I know."

The leaves of Yggdrasil rustle under a sudden forceful wind followed by the ground shaking lightly.

Mead drips from Thor's beard as he lowers the

cup from his mouth. He trains his eyes on the outside. "Is that your dragon?" He stands and twists his head to the side, undoubtedly searching for a clearer view of the door. "Oh please, let it be your dragon. I'm in the mood for an eating competition."

My sight falls to the scattered mess in front of him. Empty plates and stripped carcasses are strewn through the food spread from one side of the table to the other.

"Haven't you eaten enough already?"

"What? No, of course not." He spreads his strong muscular arms out wide. "This is a feast. Nothing is better at a feast than an eating competition, and there is no better opponent than your dragon." His eyes turn hopefully to the door again. "Is it your dragon?"

I roll my eyes and speak her name, "Elan?"

Her voice sounds in my head. *Oh, I am in. I'm so in*, she repeats.

"You two are terrible. You shouldn't be encouraging him."

She sounds offended. *Hey, he's the one who asked for me.*

Anticipation fills Thor's face as he waits.

I release a deep sigh. "She says you're on." My voice lacks enthusiasm.

Thor stands, hoisting his fist. "Yes!"

I shake my head in disbelief. "I don't know why you two don't just talk to each other."

Ignoring me, the god of thunder flexes his muscles and yells, "Bring out the cows!"

The room falls silent, and he points at the door.

"An eating competition is on!"

A loud cheer erupts, and the hall empties to the outside.

Elan's golden scales shimmer in the moonlight as she eyes the exiting warriors, searching for Thor. Within moments, two cow carcasses are brought out. One raw, with the skin on, and the other cooked to perfection. Elan stands over the raw cow, her wings tucked by her sides, posture ready, and determination set on her face. Large teeth shine through her parted lips as she challenges Thor with her eyes. She tosses her head, swinging her horns menacingly in a gesture of battle. A deep hunger burns in her eyes.

Opposite her, Thor stands over his cooked carcass almost the size of his table. He rubs his hands together, eyeing the cow and rubbing his belly before grinning at Elan. The light from the hall shines behind him, highlighting his red hair and thick beard, making them appear to be on fire. A roar of support bursts through the crowd as he shuffles his feet from side to side as if readying himself for a fight. He is not the most handsome god, but his loyal heart and dedication to charge into a battle first have won him the support of his warriors. He sits his stocky form on the chair and pulls out his dagger, ready.

I face Elan. "You don't have to do this, you know. Even though he's already had some dinner, he has a solid reputation for eating a lot."

Elan scoffs. *Pfft. Don't be ridiculous. When would I ever refuse a free meal? Besides, I can beat him.*

I tilt my head to the side. "This competition has been close in the past."

You don't have to rub it in. This time, it's going to be different. I'm starving! She nudges me with her nose, pushing me toward the spectators. *Go on. Announce that I'm ready.*

I face Thor, amazed at how he could still consider starting an eating competition after everything he has already consumed.

He wipes the smug smile off his face, and a firm determination sets in. "Well? Is she ready?"

I nod. A loud cheer reverberates through the crowd. The god of thunder thumps his fists wide on the table, one holding his dagger, point up, ready to go. I raise my hands, indicating for the crowd to quiet. It takes a while for the group to fall silent.

Every warrior and serving Valkyrie circles Elan and Thor.

After waiting a moment, I begin the countdown. "Three, two, one, begin."

Elan plants a foot on the cow's leg and rips into its body with her teeth, tearing out large chunks, swallowing them after a few chews. Thor cuts away at the cooked meat with his dagger before sinking his teeth into it and ripping out large mouthfuls. The speed with which he devours the flesh is astonishing, especially considering his stocky form is much smaller than Elan's.

Within fifteen minutes, the golden dragon consumes her carcass. After only another five minutes, Thor devours the flesh on his.

Puffing out his chest, Thor stands and wipes his beard with his arm, knocking the remaining mess from his mouth. He rubs his belly and cries, "More!"

A cheer erupts from the crowd.

The young Valkyries from the academy clean Thor's table before bringing out two more carcasses, one raw for Elan and the other cooked for Thor. Other Valkyries, winged and wingless, dart through the mix of einherjar and divine warriors, refilling their cups of mead. As they bustle, I take in the faces of the young Valkyries from the academy. They are unknown to me, as I graduated from Valkyrie Academy two years ago.

Long folds of light-blue fabric sway near the entrance of Valhalla Hall, and I'm surprised to find Mistress Sigrun propped up against a wall. Her arms are crossed over her chest, her face an array of strange amusement. She looks so different. She has replaced the Valkyrie uniform with an elegant one-strap dress that hangs from her left shoulder, displaying her muscular arms. The fabric hugs her thin figure and flows down to her ankles. Her blond hair falls in a braid down her back. She is a picture of beauty. Even though she is much older than I am, she has the Valkyrie blessing of eternal youth. Only a few slight creases betray her age. Her off-duty face looks relaxed—a strange sight to see, even though it's an expression I've seen more often recently.

My focus returns to the eating competition. I stare in disbelief as they devour the second cow. Elan tears at the raw cow flesh, each bite slightly slower than the last, yet somehow, Thor continues eating, managing to keep up with her.

Mead sloshes on my foot and seeps into my leather shoes, distracting me from the competition. My toes are wet and sticky.

"Sorry." A young, nervous wingless Valkyrie eyes

me and cowers, as though waiting to be reprimanded.

Despite feeling uncomfortable and annoyed, I smile at her. "It's okay."

She dashes off, almost at a run, and I sigh. In the last couple of years, there have been rumors of my success, blowing me up into some kind of hero. I often find it makes the young ones nervous. Me a hero? That's rubbish. It all started because I didn't want to grow up as just a servant. I guess, really, I was working toward my own interests. I'm just glad it expanded to help others also.

"What's going on?" Hildr joins me. Her spiky red hair is not much different in color than Thor's, but it's much better kept. Her freckles stand out on her pale skin in the light. Her green eyes follow the commotion. A trickle of sweat runs down her neck, and she wears her leather fighting uniform. She faces me, and the sword strapped to her side clicks against a metal buckle on her belt. She looks as though she's just finished a round of combat training.

"Thor challenged Elan to another eating competition."

A giggle sounds on my other side. "Oh, Elan would love that." Eir's peaceful face fills with joy at the sight of a dragon and a god getting along.

It's been a couple of years since the dragon alliance

was revised and the dragons were released from slavery by the gods and the Valkyries. But the peacekeeper, Eir, is always happy to see this physically in motion.

The peaceful wingless Valkyrie's pale-brown hair is back in a ponytail, and she is also wearing leather —a very unusual sight for her.

"Have you been combat training with Hildr?"

Eir nods, her eyes serious.

"And me." Britta stands on the other side of Hildr.

My jaw drops. "Eir, how uncharacteristic of you."

Combat training is a usual pastime for Hildr and Britta, especially since Odin changed his attitude about wingless Valkyries. Still, Eir has always despised fighting or anything less than peaceful.

Eir sighs. "I know, but I need to practice my battle skills, too, just in case. After all, I am a Valkyrie."

I place a hand on her shoulder. "And a very good one at that."

"Who's winning?" Britta asks, wiping sweat off her forehead.

I study the contents of both the carcasses. Both contestants seem to be slowing down.

"I don't know. It seems to be a tie."

"And who's that?" Britta nods, and I follow her gaze.

In the distance, a group of warriors gathers. A blond muscular god with a kind face stands in the middle. They are all entirely under the influence of mead, and they joke and slap each other around. The blond seems to be the center of attention. He puffs out his broad chest, and in the dim light, he appears to have a soft glow about him.

I shrug. "That's the god Balder, one of Odin's sons."

Her eyebrows rise. "I've heard about him. I thought they were exaggerating. He's so handsome," she swoons.

I roll my eyes when I look at her. Her eyes are open wide, and she twiddles the end of her hair.

"Seriously?" I shake my head. Then I remember that he seems to get that reaction from all the Valkyries. "He's married."

She grins. "That can change. These gods seem to go through a lot of wives." Suddenly her smile drops. "What are they doing?"

Returning my gaze to the group, I find that they have stepped back, leaving a large opening in the middle. On one side, Balder stands with his arms open wide. On the other side, a warrior raises a bow and arrow and points it at him. The rest of the warriors stand aside, watching, grinning.

"I thought he was well-liked." Britta's voice is shrill.

"He is," I say.

"Then why is that archer pointing an arrow at him?"

The archer draws the string back with the arrow nocked. A moment later, he releases his fingers and sets the arrow free—aiming directly for Balder.

Britta screams.

Chapter Two

B ritta charges forward, aiming for the group of warriors. I clasp her arm just in time, and she moves to shake me off.

I croon to her, "Wait."

She frowns.

"Trust me."

She spins to look at the handsome god with a kind face.

The arrow's aim is true. It hits Balder directly in the heart then falls to the ground. The group laughs, Balder joining them.

Britta's mouth drops open. "What?"

I smile. "It's one of the god's favorite party tricks."

"What on Vanir? Why?" she stammers.

"Balder had a dream that he would be harmed, and when he told Odin, word got back to Frigg, his mother. She made everything promise not to hurt him. Now everything that should be able to harm or kill Balder bounces off him. These warriors have no intention of hurting him. They do this because it amuses them that these things can't harm him."

Britta crosses her arms over her chest. "What a stupid game." She huffs. "Men."

"Indeed," I agree.

Kara.

I spin around, searching for the owner of the voice in my head. It was deeper, more mature than Elan's, and I know Elan is too busy trying to out-eat Thor to talk to me. Her mind is on one track only. As I gaze in the distance, in the opposite direction of the competition, golden scales glisten in the moonlight, catching my eye.

I call over my shoulder to my three friends still engrossed in the eating competition, "I'll be back soon. Eingana wants to chat."

I weave through the crowd and approach the dragon. "Eingana, what brings you here?"

Certainly not the eating contest my daughter is competing in. She shakes her head, gazing at Elan and Thor. She shrugs. *At least it builds relationships with the gods of Asgard, but it's not the way I would have done it.*

The image of the leader of the dragons partaking in an eating competition fills my head, and my mouth quirks with amusement. "I'm certain that it's not." I have only known this dragon to be responsible.

Eingana's gaze returns to me and catches the expression on my face before I can wipe it away. *Oh. You find that amusing, do you?*

I toss my hands out to the side and shrug. "Well, you're always so serious, and at one point, you threatened to eat me."

She tilts her head and gazes down at me with one eye. *Indeed.*

"What brings you here?" I ask again.

Even though Asgard has changed the alliance with the dragons, Eingana rarely makes a social visit.

The leader of the dragons sits on her haunches, the scales between her horns puckering in the form of a dragon frown. *It's Odin. While undergoing my surveillance of Asgard, I spotted him at the entrance of the world tree that he uses to access Mimir's well.*

"What's so unusual about that? I've heard that he goes there often to consult with the wisdom of Mimir's head. Why wouldn't he? He relinquished his eye in exchange for the wisdom."

This time it's different.

"How?"

He's writhing on the ground, screaming troubling things.

I place my hands on my hips. "So why tell me? Shouldn't his sons and the gods be told first?"

She lowers her head, staring intently into my eyes. *You know how proud he is and how he needs to appear in control.* She gazes over my shoulder at the rowdy crowd. *I don't think they are the right people to tell, especially right now.*

I peer over my shoulder at the group. Adding to the eating competition, Tyr and an einherjar are starting a mead-drinking competition.

"No. They aren't. Let's go."

Eingana squats so I can climb on, and I balk. This will be the first time I have ridden on her back. In fact, I haven't seen anyone riding the dragon ruler of Asgard's wastelands.

As though sensing my hesitance, she encourages, *Come. Climb on.*

She doesn't have to ask me twice. I climb up her saddleless back and press my legs around her neck, her golden scales digging into my flesh. It's been a while since I've ridden Elan bareback, and the memories flood back to me. Leaning forward, I clasp Eingana's golden scales as she pushes into the sky. The steady motion of her wings flapping speaks to my soul.

Ever since the dragons found me and I took my first ride, I knew where I wanted to stay—right on the back of my best friend. In this case, it's her mother, and that is almost as good.

The flight is short. The entrance of the world tree to Mimir's well is located on the other side of Yggdrasil. We circle the tree, and I spot Odin's form hunched over, on his knees, his face planted on the ground. He looks so small and dejected that it takes a moment for me to realize it is the authoritative god.

Eingana lands with a soft thud, yet the god still doesn't look up. Odin was nasty to me in the past, but looking at him like this, I can't leave him. I survey the surroundings, just in case he was attacked. Although his spear, Gungnir, lies next to him on the ground, it's better to be safe than sorry.

Cautiously, I approach him and place a hand on the back of his shoulder. "Great Odin."

An unintelligible mutter rises from his form, and he rocks.

"Great Odin," I say again, slightly louder.

Suddenly, he sucks in a large breath and sits on his heels, turning panicked eyes on me. His shoulder-length gray hair sticks out from the sides of his head as he grabs my arm with a vice grip. Instantly I feel the bruise coming.

"His children. We haven't contained his children."

I frown. "Whose children?"

"Loki's. Mimir has predicted that they shall be the

beginning of Ragnarok, and they have recently found out about their father and where he is tied. They're out for blood."

My frown deepens. "But the gods changed Vali into a vicious wolf, and he killed his brother, Narfi, Loki and Sigyn's son. They used Narfi's entrails to tie Loki under the serpent. Remember?" I screw up my nose at the thought.

His grasp on my arm tightens to the point I almost scream. "No. His other children to the giantess Angrboda."

"Who are they?"

"Jormungundr."

"The Midgard Serpent?" I scrunch my chin with my hand, trying to work out how that happened.

Odin nods. "Hel."

I squash my lips together. "The weirdo goddess that rules Niflheim?"

He nods again. "And the big hound, the one they call Fenrir."

My forehead pinches into a frown. "I didn't know he was Loki's son. He snarled at me today. Tyr said he's been acting up lately."

"That's why." His piercing blue eye turns fervent. "The children must be stopped."

I contemplate, trying to process the information.

"But other than Fenrir being a little out of sorts, none of them have caused us any trouble."

Odin waves a hand dismissively. "That doesn't matter. Mimir has predicted that these three will wreak havoc on Asgard and even aspire to take over as leaders. Take me to Thor." Odin pushes up from the ground and instantly fails to stand. His face pales.

I hold him steady. "I don't think that's wise, especially considering the condition Thor is in right now. I think we need to take you to bed, and I'll tell Thor as soon as possible."

Odin protests, "But I need to tell him."

I keep my hand on his chest, holding him in his seated position. "I'll tell him as soon as I get the opportunity." I hook my arm through his and lift him off the ground. "Come on. I'm going to help you safely to your bed."

Chapter Three

When I return to the eating competition, Thor and Elan are at the end of a carcass. I move next to an einherjar. The warrior's massive form towers over mine. He crosses his arms over his chest, and his mead bounces around in his cup as he laughs.

I rise to my tippy-toes. "What number is this one?"

He gazes at me from under bushy brown eyebrows, and his mouth moves just as a loud cheer erupts through the crowd, blocking out his answer.

"How many?" I yell.

He holds up two fingers.

I nod my thanks. They're slowing down. I work my way through the crowd to stand near my friends, inching between Hildr and Eir in the front row of spectators.

Elan's eyes meet mine. She just beat Thor in that

round, yet her victory is quiet. She looks full, her eyes drowsy, a giveaway only because she's my best friend. My beautiful golden dragon companion raises her head high and stands to attention, ready to go through another round. She won't have to go hunting for a while.

Another loud cheer explodes through the group. Thor stands, pushing his belly out and rubbing it in large, exaggerated circles as he swallows his last mouthful. Pieces of meat stick to his red beard, and he wipes them away with his arm before unbuckling his belt and hanging it over the back of his chair. The crowd falls silent as the god raises his hands.

He arches a hairy orange eyebrow, leveling his gaze on Elan. "Are you ready to go again, dragon?"

Elan nods once, her golden scales catching in the light of the building.

The god stretches and glares competitively at Elan. He tilts his head. "Okay." He raises his voice. "Let's go again."

Again, the crowd shouts their enthusiasm. I blink at Thor in disbelief.

Hildr scratches her head. "I can't believe these two are still going."

The Valkyries bring out the next cows, and I survey the crowd still coaxing them on. "Two was Thor's limit before. How does this Aesir think he's going to finish three, especially after he has already eaten at the feast?"

Eir gasps. "Thor's already eaten?"

"Yep."

After several more minutes, Elan takes a lazy mouthful of her carcass, and Thor's chewing becomes much slower than before. Slowly, Elan drops to her haunches before taking another bite then gazes sluggishly at me.

Who is winning? Elan's eyes almost show defeat. *Have I eaten more than Thor?*

I reassess the two carcasses. "I don't know. It looks about even."

She rips off a leg then swallows it whole. It takes a while to get past her throat, and her eyes appear to be swimming. *How about now?*

I double-check what's remaining of Thor's cow. "It looks like you're ahead now, a whole leg ahead."

She groans. *Finally.* She pulls back from the remainder of the cow. *I'm done.*

Thor notices and calls out across the distance, "What's the matter, dragon? Are you finished?"

Elan nods.

Thor's torpid eyes assess the two cows, and he slowly takes another bite. It's evident that he's struggling, too, but his competitive side shines forth. He slowly eats another few mouthfuls. The minutes tick by until eventually he lies back in his seat. "I'm pretty close. What's the score so far?" he asks one of the warriors standing next to him.

The einherjar walks up to Elan's carcass and assesses the amount while one of the Valkyries from the academy does the same to Thor's.

Hildr rubs her palms down her leather pants. "It looks pretty close. Don't you think?"

"You're about even," the warrior says.

Thor pushes up from the backrest on his seat. "That won't do." And he eats another five mouthfuls, each one clearly more painful than the last. He barely swallows the last mouthful then points at Elan. "See, dragon. I beat you."

Elan looks mournfully down at her carcass and shakes her head. *It's not worth the pain.*

Thor stands and cries victory. Suddenly his face turns green, and he runs from the gathered warriors to empty the contents of his stomach.

Elan tilts her head. *Is that allowed? I don't think that's permitted. If it's not approved, then I've won.*

I approach Elan and rub her snout. "I know, Elan. I certainly think you won, but consider his size. He's much smaller than you."

She lowers herself down to her stomach and groans. *I guess you're right. I'm not moving for another week.*

Mead sloshes over the edges of their pewter cups as the crowd clinks in celebration of Thor's win, then they disburse and head back inside. Loud slaps reverberate off Thor's back as the einherjar congratulate the god of thunder as they pass, giving little consideration as he continues to empty his stomach onto the garden.

After the crowd clears, I wait for Thor to finish being sick before hooking my arm in his. Hildr mirrors me on his other side. "Come on, Thor. It's time to go home."

He swings his hand dismissively at me, his body still lurching over the garden. "No, no. I'm fine. Just take me back inside. I have a victory celebration to lead." His words slur, and his breath smells of mead and vomit.

I screw up my nose and breathe through my mouth. "I'm pretty sure you're done for tonight. Come. Let's go. You can celebrate again soon."

He mutters something disagreeable under his breath and starts to struggle toward the hall before stumbling. Hildr and I hold him steady.

"What would I do without you two, especially you, Kara?"

"Actually, I was wondering if you would let me go, Thor."

He lifts his head, and it wobbles from side to side

as he attempts to look at me through slushy eyes. "Whadoya mean?" His words garble.

"Well, Odin said that you needed me when he sent me to be by your side. I thought he meant that you needed me to help you defeat Asgard's enemies. The last couple of years have been… interesting, but I've basically just been your servant."

We reach the palace and make our way up the stairs, a feat that proves difficult with a sizeable drunken warrior, and I'm glad for Hildr's help.

Thor shakes his head and raises a finger as though ready to disagree. We sway slightly.

I brace myself, steeling my core, and cut him off before he starts muttering something indecipherable. "Okay. A Valkyrie companion."

He pats me on the back. "Yeah. You're my Valkyrie companion. I love having my Valkyrie coommpannnion around," he slurs.

My mouth lifts in a one-sided smile. "That's nice, and you do treat me better than Odin used to, but I was hoping for more. I want to help Asgard, not just be a companion."

"Aww." He pinches my cheek again, roughing it like an old woman does to a child. "But I love having a Vallkyyrrie friend." His words are hard to understand, but I know he means well.

We reach Thor's level, and Hildr gives me a good-luck smirk.

I smile at Thor, his blurry eyes still trained on me. "You're drunk. Let's talk about this tomorrow." I take him through his door and into his bedroom.

"I'm not drunk. I'm sober. Let's drink more mead."

I pat him on the back, and with Hildr, I help him down to his bed and remove his boots. "Sure. Let's do that. Tomorrow. Okay?"

He holds up a finger. "I'll hold you to that."

I smirk, knowing he won't remember a thing. "Tomorrow. Your father also wants me to tell you something, but it can wait until tomorrow too." I pull a blanket over him and shake my head. It always amazes me how a grown man, or god in this case, can act like a child when drunk. With a heavy heart, I walk away with Hildr.

"I thought you loved being by Thor's side." Hildr watches me as we walk back to the hall.

"I do, and he has been kindhearted and encouraging to me. Except he often uses me too much as a Valkyrie companion. There haven't been many wars in the last couple of years to put my skills to use. Since they locked Loki away, there hasn't been much disruption or mischief. I want to do more with my life, and even though Thor is an excellent warrior, I feel as though my training is being neglected."

Hildr nods, her face full of understanding. "What did you need to tell Thor from his father? Was it about where Eingana took you?"

I look directly into Hildr's eyes. "Don't tell anyone, but I found Odin in a state near the entrance to Mimir's well. Apparently, it's prophesized that Loki's children are going to avenge Loki."

"What children?"

"He has three children from a giantess. They are Fenrir, Tyr's hound, the Midgard Serpent, and Hel."

"What?" Her jaw drops.

"Yeah. I know."

"If it's true, you know that your life with Thor is about to change. In fact, I wouldn't mind joining him myself if all that is about to begin."

- Chapter Four -

Where's the big cheater? Elan flaps her wings in frustration, lifting her front feet off the ground. She hops on her hind legs before slamming them back to the ground. The early-morning sun catches in her eyes, and they ignite with color, making them seem as though they are on fire.

"Now, Elan. You know he's not a cheater." I tilt my head to the side and gaze at her under a raised eyebrow.

Yeah, yeah. I get it. He's a puny god, and I'm a big dragon. Of course I can eat more than him. Irritation laces her tone, and her words are crisp. *I'm supposed to be able to eat more than he can. Whatever. I don't care. He should be here by now.*

"What's gotten into you today, Elan? Did you sleep on the wrong side of a rock?"

Ha, ha. Very funny. The emperor dragon swings

her head from side to side, sarcasm oozing from her voice.

Three thumps sound on the ground behind me, and the ground shakes. I turn to find Naga, Drogon, and Tanda tucking their wings by their side as their riders, Hildr, Eir, and Britta, dressed in black leather fighting attire, slide off their backs.

"Hey, guys. What brings you here?" I ask.

Hildr kicks the dirt with the toe of her shoe and looks at the ground. "Um. I kind of told them about the three children."

My cheeks turn numb with shock, and I lean closer to Hildr to eliminate anyone else hearing. "You didn't mention Odin's meltdown, did you?"

She shook her head. "I only told them about the children and the havoc they could cause. We're here because we want to help."

Elan's snarky voice sounds in my head, dragging my attention away from the wingless Valkyries. *You didn't let me finish. Mother has told us about what Odin said. That's why I'm so irritable this morning.*

I plant a hand on my hip, facing her. "Oh. It's not because you've got a bellyache from eating so many cows?"

She shakes her scaly head. *Nope. Not at all. The dragons are here to help round up Fenrir, just in case he decides to run or cause any trouble. First, though, we need to get Thor out of bed. Where is he?* She stares at the palace.

Naga's seen him. Naga snuck by his room this morning and saw him sound asleep on his bed. Naga's blue eyes are wide, displaying naivete. *Naga snuck away before Thor knew Naga was there.*

I stare at Naga with wide eyes. At first, I want to write off what he said as bad language skills, but then I remember that his communication has improved immensely over the last couple of years. "Okay." I hesitate, trying to place myself in Naga's shoes before judging. "That's an interesting thing to do, Naga."

Eir chuckles, rubbing her dragon around the ears then down his snout, and Naga nudges her with his head affectionately.

"It's been Naga's favorite thing lately. I know it's a little strange." The wind blows wisps of Eir's brown hair over her eyes, and she grins, peering through the strands. "But I am okay with that. He's only watching them sleep." She cups her hands around her mouth and whispers in my ear, "Between you and me, I think he's trying to find me a nice partner, you know, one who doesn't snore." She giggles and shrugs. "Don't ask me why. I think he thinks I'm getting old."

Naga's big blue eyes blink slowly, making him

look innocent. *Eir is aging. Eir is over twenty years. She must find a man before she gets too old. That's how it works in the dragon world.*

Eir rubs his ear again and presses her side braid against his scales. "Oh, Naga. How many times do I have to tell you? Valkyries live a very long time. On top of that, they also look young for a very long time. Look at Mistress Sigrun."

Naga shivers, like something ran down his spine. *No, thank you.*

Someone nudges my back, and I turn to find Elan's golden eyes level with mine. *Come on. That's enough time wasted. Just because he's a god doesn't mean he can keep us waiting.*

"Actually, Elan, it does mean he can keep us waiting, but let's give it a try anyway. Thor can be a bit more lenient than other gods around here, and it is a matter of importance."

We trek up toward a segment of Odin's palace. The massive balcony off Thor's bedroom makes it hard to miss. Elan lands on the open part of the balcony and crouches to her stomach. I climb off her back as she ducks her head under the eaves and peers in the window.

I try the door, find it unlocked, and ease my way in. Thor's large form lies sprawled across a king-size bed framed with thick posts in each corner. Red curtains drape from the beams. His body is spread expansively, instantly explaining why he sleeps alone and not with his wife. Lack of space would be a big enough deterrent, let alone the earth-rumbling snore that bellows from the depths of his body.

Dragon scales! Would you look at that? Elan tilts her head, her mouth filling the doorway, and breathes out a plume of steam.

Instantly my skin becomes damp with sweat. "Elan, stop," I hiss. "What are you doing?"

Her golden eye looks eerie as she peers through the small window at me. *I'm waking him up. Isn't that what we're here for?*

I shake my head with disbelief. "There are nicer ways to do it."

You're right, although he looks pretty out of it. Her window-framed eye looks at Thor. *I was just trying to help.*

"Thanks, I guess, but let me try first."

Elan harrumphs. *Fine. Whatever. Good luck.*

I gaze at the snoring Thor. A slight sheen of sweat coats his skin after Elan filled his room with steam, and still, he hasn't moved an inch.

Sitting on the edge of his bed, I lightly shake his shoulder. "Thor. Wakey, wakey." He doesn't budge. "Thor, wake up," I say in a singsong voice.

Loud snores answer me, interrupted only when

he rubs his nose and flicks his arm to the side, narrowly missing me.

See. I told you, Elan chides, her snout barely fitting into the door of his room.

I glare at her eye peering through the window.

All right, all right. I get it. Quiet!

I shake the sleeping god harder, moving his torso roughly from side to side, yet he still doesn't stir. Raising my voice, I call, "Thor. Wake up!" A groan escapes my lips as I'm answered with more snores. My shoulders slump, and I spot a spare pillow on the other side of the bed. With a spring in my step, I work my way around the posts and grab it, restraining myself slightly when I hit him over the head. "Wake up."

Thor mutters something, grumbles, and turns to the other side. I let out an exasperated sigh before following him to the other side and whacking him with the pillow. Thor snorts and works his mouth loudly before progressing with his snores.

"Vanir! This man can sleep." I gaze at Elan, feeling lost.

Excitement fills Elan's eye. *Can I help now?*

I shrug. "Sure. Why not?"

A grin spreads across her mouth, framed by the doorway, giving her a conniving look. She twists her mouth to the side farther and shoves it through the door. *Okay. Ready yourself. This could be uncom-fortable.*

I frown. "What do you me—"

I'm cut off by Elan's voice blasting through my head, followed by a puff of hot air. *Wake up!*

I jump. Next to me, Thor flies out of bed, grabbing his hammer from his bedside, and stands at attention. His bare chest heaves with anticipation as he surveys his surroundings, dressed in his boxer shorts. His eyes are wide, and his muscles flex as he waves Mjollnir threateningly until his eyes land on me pressing my back against the wall, trying to keep out of his hammer's reach. "Kara?"

Elan snorts through the door, and Thor spins and cries out, puffing and holding his spare hand over his heart when he spots Elan's eye through the window. "Argh! You two are going to be the death of me."

Elan smiles, exposing her extensive array of sharp teeth, managing to look more scary than friendly. *Glad I could help.*

Thor sets Mjollnir on the floor. "What is the meaning of this?" He searches for some clothes and pulls on leather pants and a tunic. He pauses, rubbing his head. "Why do I feel so terrible?"

Ah. That was me, Elan says. *I beat you in an eating competition.*

I scowl at Elan.

Thor rubs his stomach and looks thoughtful. "Really?"

Yep. Elan's eyes dance with mischief.

"Hmph! We'll just have to have another run, won't we? Not right now, though. I expect you feel just as terrible as I do."

Um—Elan looks at me, and I frown at her—*sure, but I guess all that mead you drank on top of it didn't help.*

Thor holds his head again before looking at me. "I guess not. Why are you two here, anyway?"

"Your father wants me to tell you something."

"Oh. What is it?"

"While you were partying last night and partaking in your eating competition, Eingana dropped by and took me to Odin. He was huddled next to the entrance of the world tree that he uses to access Mimir's well, overcome with a vision. He was quite distressed, and he needs us to deal with it right away."

"What do we need to deal with?" Thor asks, pulling on some strings to tighten his clothes and securing some bands over his arms.

"He had a vision that Loki's children from his giant mistress, Angrboda, are going to cause havoc."

"Do you mean Fenrir, Jormungundr, and Hel?" Thor asks.

"So, you know about them?" I ask hesitantly.

"My father sent two of them to the ends of the realm to try to keep them out of trouble. He sent Jormungundr to Midgard, and the beast circles the oceans there. He sent Hel to the realm of the shameful dead because she prefers their company. And last of all, we kept Fenrir here because, as you know, he's a puppy, and he's so adorable. What's the problem that my father saw?" Thor secures the final strap on his clothes and armor.

"He's worried because Loki's children just found out what happened to him. Somehow the information was delayed in getting to them. I think he might be right. Last night, I ran into Fenrir with Tyr. Fenrir wasn't friendly. He growled at me and was quite cranky. It's not the way I remember him. With him being so big now, it was quite disturbing. He needs to be contained."

Thor's shoulders sag. "Fine. I'll chain him, and we can monitor him from there."

Is that your answer to everything? Elan snaps. *You gods love your chains.*

Thor spins to look at her one eye peering through the window. "It's not the answer for everything, just when something is dangerous and needs to be restrained before it hurts anyone. I'm sure Tyr will look after Fenrir and let him off occasionally."

Elan huffs.

Thor shakes his head. "But first, we must see if we can chain him. It's a simple solution." He walks toward the door and opens it. "Are you coming, Kara? Or shall I meet you outside?"

"I'll meet you outside in a couple of minutes," I call over my shoulder as I follow Elan's snout onto the balcony.

- Chapter Five -

"Where's Thor?" Hildr calls to me before Elan lands.

Elan's body shudders underneath me as her feet hit the ground before my wingless Valkyrie friends and their dragons.

"He's coming," I say, climbing off her back.

Chains rattle behind me, and the faces of Naga, Drogon, and Tanda drop as their eyes widen. I follow their line of sight and spot Thor carrying massive chains draped across his arms. With every movement he makes, the chains clang together.

Thor eyes each of the dragons' expressions, and the small amount of face showing above his bushy red beard softens. "Oh. It's all right, you fantastic beasts. It's not going to be the same as when you were chained. Tyr will look after Fenrir and hopefully tame him so we can remove these soon."

Drogon huffs steam. *Then you won't mind if the dragons supervise. Let us be the ones who decide that.*

Thor chuckles. "Be my guest. I promise you it's all above board. I've known Fenrir since he was a pup, and Tyr is my brother. He adores Fenrir. I wouldn't want to jeopardize that." Gazing at the dragons in front of him, his muscles strain as he holds up the chains. "Would one of you mind carrying these, please?" His eyes land on Drogon, and he studies the many horns on the dragon's head. "Drogon. Would you mind carrying them? They could easily rest across your horns."

Drogon looks displeased, and his eyes carry distrust as he huffs another plume of steam. *As long as you abide by your word and let us supervise. We're not going to let something happen to Fenrir like it did to us.*

Thor smiles, showing off his straight white teeth between his bushy red beard and mustache. "Of course. It's exactly as I just agreed. I have no interest in treating any animal with cruelty. However, a dangerous animal must be contained, especially if it's going to be a threat to Asgard."

Drogon lowers his head, and Thor drapes the chains over his many horns.

"In fact, I suggest we get Tyr to make it into a game for Fenrir."

As a group, we set out to find Tyr, following Thor

to the spot where the gods usually like to spar. The clashing of weapons greets us as we near. Following the sound, we find several gods deep in battle against each other.

"Ah," Britta moans. "If I'd known where you were going, I could have waited for you here."

I follow her line of sight until my eyes fall on Balder in the corner sparring with Tyr. I roll my eyes. Balder catches sight of us and waves, flashing an impressive smile that I'm sure would win many maidens' hearts. While the friendly god is distracted, Tyr's muscles ripple down his bare arms as he swings his sword at Balder. The sword swipes across the invincible god's torso, cutting the material yet leaving Balder's skin unscathed. If Balder weren't protected against all items, he would have been severely injured. The difference between this day and the party is this was not executed as a joke.

Balder pulls his gaze from us and glances down at Tyr's sword as though it were a distraction before fighting Tyr back, his friendly face relaxed and unthreatening as he practices with the god of war. The muscles in his exposed torso flex as he swings his sword.

Britta expels a loud, swooning sigh.

"Tyr!" Thor calls.

The god of war pauses of his battle and looks up, his questioning eyes squinting through sweat.

"Can we talk for a minute?" Thor's eyes travel to Fenrir, sleeping in the corner.

The hound opens one eye, watching Tyr's every move, and his ears twitch, twisting in the direction of the two gods. Moving farther away from the hound, the two gods lean their heads closer together, their mouths barely moving and their voices low.

Worry covers Tyr's face until eventually he slaps Thor on the shoulder and pulls back. "And a game it shall be." He gazes at the hound and calls, "Fenrir!"

The hound leaps to his feet and runs to Tyr, his long bushy tail wagging as though he were a pup called by his best friend.

"Yes, Tyr?" Fenrir's friendly gaze fills with distrust and curiosity as he glances at Thor, the dragons, and their riders.

Tyr pets Fenrir on his shoulder. "We want to see if you're stronger than a dragon."

Instantly the scruffy hound's eyes fill with excitement. Fenrir sits on his haunches with his back straight, and he's taller than any of the gods. The dragons still loom over his bulky, intimidating form.

"This sounds like fun." His long brown tail wags.

Thor retrieves the chains from Drogon's horns

and carries them to Fenrir. The wolf's eyes widen with surprise, and he retreats slightly.

"Don't fear, Fenrir. These are the chains that held the dragons captive. The dragons think that they are the strongest creatures around." He challenges Fenrir with his gaze. "If you're happy to agree with that, then that's your burden to bear."

The four dragons puff out their chests, and Fenrir's furry eyebrows crowd his eyes, displaying his displeasure.

Thor nods at him. "If you want to see if you're stronger than the dragons, then let us place these on you to prove that you are indeed the strongest creature."

The dragons huff, showing their distain at the notion.

Fenrir's gaze falls on each of the dragons, taking in their displeased faces. His mouth forms into a strange smirk, exposing his big teeth, and he moves closer to Thor. "I'd love to have a go. It sounds fun."

Balder and Tyr help Thor drape the chains around Fenrir's throat and secure the chains to a boulder. Thor pulls and pushes against the chains and their anchor, testing the strength of the attachment. The connection doesn't budge.

Tyr turns to Fenrir, a challenging grin plastered

on his face. "Okay, Fenrir. You're on. Let's see what you got."

Fenrir pulls and strains, stretching out his neck and shoulders, hunkering down and pushing with his haunches. The chains clank against the stone several times, the heavy metal whooshing as it swings wildly from the test. Moments later, the chains snap, and the metal clunks to the ground and clangs against the rock boulder.

Fenrir stands tall, his face filled with victory and pride. "Look at me, dragons. I'm stronger than you. Look at the chain you couldn't escape lying broken on the ground."

Drogon's displeased eyes narrow on me. *Is this guy kidding? The dragons didn't break free because they were protecting the alliance, not because we couldn't.*

I try to look understanding while holding my finger to my lips in a shushing motion.

Elan picks up on my sentiment. *We know, Drogon. This is just a game. Relax. All of the dragons were bound by the alliance and did not flee because of that.* She nods to Fenrir, her golden-brown eyes filling with worry. *But you must admit, he's strong, and that is worrisome.*

Drogon nods.

Tyr claps his hands in approval. "Well done, Fenrir. You beat the dragons."

Tanda's grumble echoes through my head, and I glance at her and wink only to be rewarded with a fiery-red glare.

"Yes, Fenrir," Thor agrees, his voice booming. "You're very strong. This was hardly a challenge at all. We'll have to make a stronger chain and see how you do next time." He spins to greet the gods. "Why don't you work on that?"

Tyr unfastens the chain around Fenrir's neck and rubs him behind the ear. Fenrir happily tilts his head to the side, his tongue drooping from his mouth.

Grabbing the remaining chains, the other gods who had gathered to spar head in the direction of the smith, their brows furrowed in confusion.

Watching them leave so soon, my shoulders slump with disappointment. "Oh, great!" I grumble. "I didn't even get to partake in anything exciting or useful today. My friends even lined up to help me." I search for Thor and spotted him heading back to the palace. "Thor!" I yell. "Can I talk to you for a minute?"

My leader turns and calls over his shoulder, "Of course, Kara!"

He pauses, and I jog to catch up with him. When I reach his side, he slaps me on the back, sending a painful jolt through my upper back, and I grit my teeth.

"What is it?" he asks.

"Well," I hesitate. "I've been meaning to ask you for a while. Do you really need me to be around?"

His red bushy eyebrows push together. "What do you mean?"

"Well, Odin sent me to help you. He said it like you needed my help."

"You are helping. You let me have competitions with your dragon."

I place my hands on my hips. "We did have this conversation last night, but you were a bit out of it."

"We did?"

I nod.

"Can you remind me?" A slight amount of sympathy enters his voice.

"I'm kind of sick of being a Valkyrie companion." I hold up my hand in a stopping motion. "Don't get me wrong. I don't mind being your friend, but I'm bored. I want to do something important with my life. The way things are going, I don't feel like I'm achieving anything."

Thor slaps me on the shoulders again, and my body lurches forward with his force. He has got to start remembering that I am much finer than he is. "Kara, Kara. You are my Valkyrie friend. Surely you know I appreciate you. Threats against Asgard have been a bit quiet of late." He shrugs. "But if what my father predicts becomes true, you're about to become a very busy Valkyrie."

"I will?" With a blank face, I stare at him. "What do you mean?"

He smirks. "For starters, you can go down to Midgard and start searching for Beowulf."

"Who's that?"

"He's a human who hasn't died in battle yet but is a great warrior. He takes down all the hideous creatures in Midgard, and he also fights spectacularly in battles."

"Okay," I say hesitantly, unsure of where this is going.

"I need you to look for him. He should know where the Midgard Serpent is. When you find Beowulf, ask him if he knows the location of the serpent, and send me a message through the world tree."

"How?" I frown.

"Call Ratatoskr. He lives in Yggdrasil and loves to spread messages. He will find me and get the message to me." He turns to leave then pauses and turns back. "Oh, and take your friends and your dragons with you. You lot work well together, and a trip will be great for you."

Chapter Six

We mount our dragons, heading to Heimdall's tower and the Bifrost portal. The large watchman stands at attention, looking out over the void, scanning for any threats. His massive body is covered in armor with a horned helmet on his head. A large sword hangs from his belt, following the length of his thigh.

After circling the gatekeeper on our dragons, we land on the large platform in front of his tower.

Elan lowers her torso to the ground, and I dismount. "Good morning, Heimdall."

Remaining in a ready stance, he pulls his gaze from the space and focuses it on me. A subtle friendliness leaks through his dark-brown irises, a change from not so long ago when he had been suspicious of my actions and my motives for wanting to go to Midgard. He remains standing at the ready, a staff propped in front of him, balanced between his large hands. Even though his gaze is friendly, his all-knowing eyes seem to peer right to the bottom of my soul.

"Good morning, Valkyries and dragons." His eyes pass over my friends. "It's been a long time since I have seen any of you come this way. Things have changed over the years." His eyes return to me.

"Yes, they definitely have changed," I agree as I weigh the differences between his greetings then and now. "And pleasant changes they are."

A slight smirk quirks his lips. "It's been a while since you have tried to sneak into Midgard. Have you lost interest now that you're allowed to go?"

I shake my head. "Thor's been keeping me busy. We're here today because he's sending us on a mission."

A small crease appears between his eyebrows. "I can't see any battles on Midgard today."

"It's not for collecting souls. He wants us to find someone on Midgard."

Heimdall lifts an eyebrow. "And who might that be?"

As I move closer, I crane my neck to look at his face. "He wants us to find Beowulf. Have you heard of him?"

He lifts his chin and lowers it slowly as though in confirmation. "Ah, yes. The great human warrior who fights against the monsters on Midgard. I will send you in his direction." In one big bound, he steps up to the portal, ready to send us through. "Kara. You and your dragon can go through first, then I will send the rest of you through individually with your dragons."

I mount Elan's back, and she stands on the portal. Heimdall pulls the lever, and the bright rainbow colors of the Bifrost flash around us before we're sucked into its portal and delivered to Midgard.

Elan lands, her feet hitting the ground with a thud that shudders through her body and rattles mine. When my vision calms from the vibration, I study my surroundings. Once again, I'm awestruck by the beauty of Midgard. This time though, the stark greenness of the land and rolling hills contrasting with the deep-blue lakes is striking. Its beauty calls to me. Filling my eyes with the greenery of the land, I ponder how strange it is to be here and not searching for the destruction of war to reap warriors' souls.

One by one, three thuds sound behind me as the rest of my small team of wingless Valkyries and dragons join us.

An insect of some sort emerges from a nearby flowering bush. Its big white wings flap slowly as it flutters past my head and lands on Eir's extended hand.

Eir squeals, her face beaming as she observes the insect. "This is what they call a butterfly. I've always wanted to see one of these. There are so many different types with many different colors." She twists her hand around to observe the white wings with a couple of black dots and the dark, almost-black body. "This one is quite bland, although it's still beautiful and fascinating. So many of their kind display vibrant colors." A dreamy expression covers her face.

The butterfly rests on her hand for a moment then lifts off, fluttering into the distance. I observe its progress until I realize there's a village snuggled not far behind the mountains.

"We should try there first." I point in the direction of the village. "It should be a perfect place to ask questions and see if they know of Beowulf."

Hildr presses her sword against her thigh as though ready for action. "Sounds like a plan."

Our dragons take flight, carrying us to the village with a few flaps of their wings, and land on a plain just outside the village.

Before we can dismount, a half-dressed man with animal leather wrapped around his waist charges us with a spear in hand. He points the spear at Elan, the closest dragon to the village, and waves it threateningly. "Begone, you terrible creatures."

Elan retracts her head and stands tall. *Who does this guy think he is?* Her voice booms in my head.

Unsure if we reached the right village and in need of information, I call, "We come in peace. These dragons will not harm you. We're searching for someone."

"These are monsters! They will slaughter our village." He crosses his forearms then thumps his chest with both fists before flexing his arms to the side, showing off his muscles. He does all of this while still managing to hold the spear in one hand.

Would you look at that? This guy has more brawn than the gods, Elan comments snidely.

The man before us puffs out his chest. "I am Beowulf. I kill these monsters for a living. None will survive me."

Elan shoots a plume of steam out of her nostrils. *Yeah, right. There's four of us and one of him.*

A strange sound reaches me from behind. Curious, I turn to see Drogon's head nodding and his lips working hard to cover his teeth. I admire him for his effort, even though he isn't very successful. Hildr must have told him how vicious a dragon looks while exposing its teeth.

"Are you laughing, Drogon?" I call over my shoulder quietly to refrain from letting Beowulf hear.

Naga looks at Drogon then at me, amusement

shining in his big blue eyes. *Yes. Drogon laughs at this man. Naga thinks he's funny too.*

I agree with them. His display was interesting, to say the least. However, I don't think laughing at him is the best idea right now. I motion with my hand, my palm facing the ground in a calming motion. "All right. Settle. This isn't helping." My voice remains slightly louder than a whisper, and I hope Beowulf doesn't hear me.

I turn to face him only to be confronted by Beowulf as he hunkers down with his spear pulled over his head, ready to throw it at the dragons.

"Beowulf!" I yell. "Thor sent us to find you. He needs your help."

Beowulf halts just before throwing, his spear poised in his hand as though he's a warrior statue. "What?" His face screws up as though he's half deaf, then his expression flattens. "But these are monsters, enemies of Beowulf. Why would Thor send monsters?"

Elan lowers her body, and I dismount to approach him.

"Thor sent his most trusted warrior maidens and the mounts they ride. These are not monsters." I indicate the dragons. "These dragons are our friends and fierce protectors to have by our sides. We have an agreement with them, and they help us protect Asgard."

Beowulf lowers his spear, his fierce face distorted with confusion.

I repeat, "I am here because Thor needs your help."

"What with?"

"We've received some news that Jormungundr might be about to wreak havoc. Thor asked me to come and see if you have noticed the Midgard Serpent acting strange and causing any trouble. Also, he wants to know if you've seen where it likes to spend most of its time."

Beowulf's face straightens, and his eyes look distant as he gazes far away. I follow his line of sight to the large body of water several miles away from his village.

"The sea is restless. We didn't know why, but this would make sense. The serpent's head has emerged every so often, and it seems to be circling Midgard. Many fishermen are missing. The fish numbers are diminishing, and the serpent appears to be growing."

"Do you think you could assist Thor in containing the serpent?" I ask, scanning his body for any sign of fear.

Beowulf puffs out his bare chest. "Beowulf doesn't back down from any challenge of defeating a monster." His chest caves slightly, yet pride remains on his face. "Although sometimes I need the help of others to do this. Thor is a worthy accomplice, and I'll be proud to help him with this."

"Wonderful," I say, my attention caught by a movement in the distance.

A massive wave careens toward the shore, evolving in size, and washes over several trees.

Eir gasps as a giant serpent's head covered with murky-brown scales emerges briefly out of the water. "This would be the perfect spot for Thor to come."

Beowulf's face looks troubled as he watches the serpent. "This is what the serpent has been doing. It must be stopped. Thor must come soon, as Jormungundr only travels this way once a moon cycle. You can see it is already here, and it will leave soon. Once gone from here, I don't know where it goes."

I mount Elan and turn to leave, calling over my shoulder, "I'll get the message to Thor!"

Beowulf nods. "Come and get me when you're ready, or perhaps your colleagues and their dragons can defeat the monster."

"Now, there's an idea." Hildr shines with enthusiasm and points at Beowulf. "I like that one."

Chapter Seven

The water in the ocean continues to swirl higher, the swell of the waves rising with the squirming serpent's body. The waves lap at the edges of several houses that line the coast, and I fear for their fate, my heart racing with apprehension over the peoples' safety.

"Come on, Elan. We need to get to Yggdrasil and find that squirrel."

Elan pushes into the air, and within moments, we're at the base of the world tree.

I stick my head inside one of the holes and call, "Ratatoskr!"

It feels stupid calling to an overgrown rodent that I've never met. I have no idea what to expect from the squirrel. Although, when I think about it, I have done far crazier things for the sake of Asgard. I trust Thor's information is correct, and I've heard rumors before about this little creature that runs up and down the world tree, delivering messages.

A loud splash sounds behind me, and I turn to see a massive wave crashing onto the shore. The slippery scales of a serpent rise then fall beneath the surface of the water. Thor needs to come down now. It's crucial that I get this message to him as soon as possible.

"Ratatoskr!" I don't know how long it could take the squirrel to get to me. Usually, squirrels are fast movers, but maybe this one is different or only comes when it suits it. I'm desperate to get this message to Thor.

I hear a loud *yahoo* behind me. Following the sound, I spot Beowulf riding on Drogon's back, his hands clasped around Hildr's waist. Their forms rise and fall with the flapping of Drogon's wings. Britta follows on Tanda's back with Naga and Eir not far behind them. They must be heading toward the Midgard Serpent. Fear twists in the depths of my stomach. The monster needs intervention, but I'm worried about them. Despite his boasting and strength, Beowulf isn't Thor. He doesn't have a magical hammer and the bonus strength of a god, especially one with Megingjord, the belt of might that doubles power.

I worry my bottom lip. Thor needs to come straightaway, and I need to get this message to him so I can join them. I can't stand the thought of my friends approaching danger without me, even if they are adept fighters with three dragons.

I call up Yggdrasil again, "Ratatoskr! Ratatoskr!"

Spinning around to check on my friends, I catch sight of Jormungundr's head rising out of the water. My jaw drops, and my cheeks turn clammy. It's huge.

A strange rustling sounds behind me, and I jump. Turning, I stare straight into the beady eyes of a little red squirrel. It's almost double the size of the typical squirrel I've seen on Midgard, and its red fur stands on end. The squirrel sits on an outside branch of the world tree. Its whiskers twitch as its nostrils sniff curiously at me. It rises to its hind legs, and its fluffy tail twitches in an agitated motion.

My forehead pinches together. "Ratatoskr?"

With crossed arms, the squirrel leans against the tree and hooks one leg in front of the other. He tilts his head to the side, wearing a curious expression. "And who asks?"

I hold a hand over my chest. "I'm Kara. I'm a Valkyrie serving under Thor."

"So, I guess you think that gives you special privileges." He flicks a hand at me while shaking his head with attitude. "You know, because you serve under Thor." His words are exaggerated and slow. He gazes over my shoulder. "Valkyries are supposed to have wings. Where are yours? Or are you just lying to me?"

I raise an eyebrow. "Where have you been? Some Valkyries have wings, and some don't. Have you been hiding under a log?" I fill my words with the same attitude that the squirrel gave me.

Ratatoskr holds out a forepaw, indicating the world tree. "Actually, I've been living under the leaves of Yggdrasil. That's kind of a log. Why are you calling me?"

"I need you to run up and tell Thor something."

"What am I, your messenger?" He places a fisted forepaw on his hip.

I arch an eyebrow. "I've heard you're a messenger, especially along the world tree."

His eyes narrow. "Yeah, I'm a messenger, but not for stupid messages like that."

I pull back my shoulders. "Thor told me to use you as our messenger."

Ratatoskr grunts. "I only carry messages with insults, not serious information."

My jaw drops. "What's the point of carrying insulting messages?"

He gazes casually at his claws. "They get the reactions I want. You should see what happens when I send a message from the eagle down to Nidhogg, the dragon, or the dragon up to the eagle. It creates all sorts of mischief." The squirrel shrugs. "I guess you could say that's my payment." He lifts his head. "I don't do these things for free."

I bunch my lips to the side. "No, I guess you don't."

A war cry erupts behind me, and I turn to see Drogon diving toward Jormungundr with Beowulf and Hildr on his back. Hildr remains in the prime seat with her sword held high, and Beowulf holds a spear poised in his hand.

I growl. They should have waited. I need to get Thor here quickly. My mind whirls, trying to think of an insult to send Thor, hoping he can read between the lines to understand the meaning behind my message. "Okay. Then, tell Thor to get his ugly butt down here. If he doesn't, then I will personally make sure every part of his body is shaven. Then we will see how tough he is when he looks like a boy."

Ratatoskr's eyebrow rises. "He's pretty hairy, isn't he?"

I nod.

He huffs and looks thoughtful. "Okay. I guess I can give you that one." The squirrel scurries up the tree, and I watch the red-furred creature jump from branch to branch, weaving in and out of the world tree leaves until he's out of sight.

Breathing a sigh of relief that a message is finally getting to Thor, I turn around and jump onto my dragon's back. "Come on, Elan. Hopefully Thor will understand the real meaning of the message. If not, then he's going to take it as an insult."

Why would he be insulted? Elan asks. *You just stated the truth.*

"Yeah, but he is a god. I'm supposed to respect him and all that."

Even so, they have to earn respect.

"He has, Elan." I laugh. "Just don't tell him that."

She takes to the sky, unfurling her gorgeous golden wings. It only takes a few minutes before we arrive at the spot where our friends hover around the Midgard Serpent. It churns under the water, its head submerged in the ocean. Elan circles the area. The serpent's eyes follow the dragons' every move.

I call to Hildr and Beowulf, "Was that really a smart idea?"

Beowulf bellows, "We had to do something before it disappeared to another section of the ocean! It would be hard to find the head again." His spear remains poised in his hand, ready to strike, as he glares at the serpent below. "As you can see, it has us in its sights now and is not about to leave."

"Yeah. It looks like it's eyeing us as prey. Great job!" Britta calls, a hint of sarcasm in her tone.

"Can't we just speak to it or sing it a song or something to calm it down?" Eir asks.

Hildr huffs. "I'm open to ideas, Eir. If you can sing it to sleep, you go right ahead."

Eir's eyes open wide. "I'm not a siren."

"Did you get the message to Thor?" Hildr calls to me.

"I hope so. It's a rather interesting squirrel."

Hildr frowns. "What do you mean?"

"He would only take the message if I sent an insult. So I'm hoping Thor gets the meaning. Has anyone gotten close to the Midgard Serpent?"

We have. Elan's voice breaks my concentration on Hildr.

I hold my breath and glance down. The dark-blue water ripples underneath us as Elan's talons barely miss the dark, looming surface. Suddenly the water pushes up from underneath, surging like a spring, higher and higher.

My heart races, and I clamp my teeth before screaming, "Elan, pull up! What are you doing? Quick! Pull up!"

Jormungundr's gaping mouth charges out of the water only a couple of feet below us, ready to swallow us whole.

Chapter Eight

E lan's enormous wings push down, the tips breaking the water's surface as her body jerks up. The ascent is slow. My stomach lurches to my throat, and my knuckles turn white as I grip her reins. I'm caught unaware and smothered in helplessness. I haven't gathered enough of my magic to throw it at the rising serpent.

The serpent's massive form rises higher, swallowing any distance we manage to create. I grit my teeth and hook my feet tightly in the stirrups. Holding out a palm toward Jormungundr, I clasp the blue rock necklace hanging around my neck with my other palm. Magic shoots out of my extended palm, transferred from the magic stored in the blue rock, and it hits the serpent in the nose.

The serpent writhes and drops to the sea, a strange strangling sound coming from its throat. I shoot another blast at the serpent, draining the last of the power within the charm necklace. The force within the second blast isn't as strong as the first, yet it's enough to sizzle the serpent's skin, causing it to contort some more.

I push the joy of seeing it retreat aside as the scaly flesh disappears under the surface, water splashing out to the sides and coating the other dragons and their riders. I hope I haven't scared it off before Thor arrives. Even though I had no other choice—it had to be done, as Elan and I weren't about to become the serpent's lunch—worry over Asgard's safety torments me.

"Don't ever do that again, Elan!" I scream at her.

Her wings continue to labor, pushing us higher and higher. *Sorry. I just wanted a closer look. Dragon scales! It's quick for such a big thing.*

We rise until we reach the level of the other dragons and hover next to them.

Britta gazes down at the serpent. "Don't you think it's weird that Loki gave us magic? We've used its power against Loki and his children." The wind from the dragons' wings blows the loose strands of her brown hair in her face, and she pushes them back to look at us. "It's rather ironic, really."

I ponder the thought. "I still haven't worked out why Loki gave us magic. It doesn't make sense. If he was planning to bring down Asgard the whole time, then why would he help make his enemy stronger?"

"It is rather weird." Eir pulls at the long braid slung over her shoulder. "Perhaps we aren't seeing the bigger picture. Maybe Loki didn't intend to hurt Asgard, and he had another reason behind raising the dragon army. We never got to see his trial."

Hildr snorts. "Eir, you have got to stop seeing the good in everyone." Hildr spreads her arms in agitation, her voice chastising. "Some are purely out to hurt others. You can't see anything good in that."

Eir raises her chin and flicks her braid over her shoulder. She clutches the strap on Naga's saddle. "I will never stop believing there is good in people and other beings. None of us can be a hundred percent evil or good. Everyone has two sides."

Hildr chuckles. "Yeah, right. All you ever show is a good side. If you have a bad side, you're hiding it well. You even hate hurting a fly."

Eir crosses her arms. "Is there something wrong with that?"

Hildr shakes her head, frustrated defeat altering her features.

Britta answers for her. "No. Eir. Just be yourself. Don't listen to her sarcasm and negativity. I think it's refreshing that you project positivity and see value in everybody."

A red glow on land catches my eye, and I glance over to see Thor on the shore, the sun illuminating his red hair from behind. A monstrous giant about twice his size stands behind him, making Thor's robust form seem puny and ungodlike. The sight brings a smile to my face.

"Haha! Beowulf!" Thor's voice carries across the water, and he punches his fist into the air. He climbs off his carriage, strung behind his two trusty goats, Tanngrisnir and Tanngnjostr.

A loud cry booms from behind Hildr, making the four of us jump. Beowulf shakes his spear, his face filled with excitement. "Thor! Haha!" Beowulf pounds his spare fist on his chest then flexes his arm, pumping it in the air. After his brief display, he thumps Hildr on the shoulder, the sound reaching my ears, then points to Thor. "Fly!"

Hildr glares over her shoulder before commanding Drogon to approach the shoreline, and we follow. Thor tramples across the grass, the giant following not far behind him.

I frown. "Any idea why he brought a giant?" I ask Elan.

Elan chuckles. *Maybe he thinks he's too small to catch such a big serpent.*

Drogon lands a few feet away from Thor, and

Beowulf hastily climbs down, bounds to Thor, and slaps him on the shoulders.

"Good to see you."

"And you," Thor replies.

"It's been a long time." Beowulf eyes the giant warily.

Elan lands a few feet behind Drogon, and I dismount. With my feet securely on the ground, I look up to find Thor studying me, a strange look in his eyes.

"Kara." Thor's voice is firm, his eyes unwavering. "I got your message. So, which part are you going to shave?" He pushes his cloak away from his front and tilts his hips forward, humor dancing in his eyes. "Are you going to shave all of me?"

An involuntary cough escapes my throat, and my eyes drop to the ground as heat rushes to my cheeks. "I had to say something to get Ratatoskr to pass on the message. He refused to carry it unless I sent you an insult."

Thor laughs, his eyes taking in every bit of my blushing face. He slaps me on the shoulder, making my body lurch forward, the pressure easing my embarrassment. "I know. I was having fun. That squirrel takes pleasure in causing others grief."

Finally, he pulls his attention away from me and focuses on his human friend. Noticing Beowulf's gaze, Thor says, "Don't worry about the giant. He's here in peace. This is Tyr's stepfather, Hymir. We're going on a fishing trip."

"You're going on a fishing trip?" Beowulf asks, his voice full of disbelief.

Hildr scans the area. "Where is your boat?"

Thor appears as though this jogged his memory. "Oh. Right. That's in the carriage." The four Valkyries look at each other for answers and frown.

Beowulf follows suit, his voice full of disbelief. "You have a boat big enough to carry you and a giant in a carriage that's pulled by goats?"

Thor shrugs. "Of course. Where else would I keep my boat?" He reaches into the carriage and pulls out a large bag before walking to the side of the ocean.

We follow, watching him pull a material out of his bag and unfold it from a compacted parcel. It grows more extensive with each unfolded section until eventually the soft material firms and forms into a large boat. He pushes it deeper as the last bit expands over the water's edge.

Beowulf's mouth sits agape. "Is this an illusion?"

An amused smirk shines from under Thor's burly red beard. "Why would you think that?"

Beowulf stares at Thor with astonishment. "You carried this on a cart that is pulled by goats. Not only that—it unfolds from a small package into a massive ship."

"Oh, that." Thor chuckles. "Of course. This is Skidbladnir. It was made especially for Frey by the dwarves, and he has loaned it to me. It's rather nifty. Not only are the dwarves crafty, but they have also forged it with magic and other witchcraft." He smiles proudly while observing the ship. "It's rather convenient, don't you think?" He pushes the boat into deeper water and climbs on, holding out his hand to the giant. "Are you coming, Hymir?"

Hymir climbs on the boat bobbing and wobbling on the water, and the color drains from the giant's face.

"Is it going to hold him?" Britta calls.

"Of course." Thor looks offended.

Unconvinced, I add, "Are you sure it's a good idea to go fishing in that boat? The serpent is rather large. The whole boat could probably fit inside its head. Trust me. I've seen it firsthand."

"Oh, Kara. See? I knew I had you around for a reason." He walks down to the end of the boat and turns a knob. Instantly the boat starts to grow, as does Hymir's confidence that the ship will hold his weight. The wobbling slows to a controlled pace.

I shake my head in disbelief. I can't believe they are planning a fishing trip while we're all here to help with the Midgard Serpent. Although the boat is impressive. "What are you fishing for?" I call.

Thor's smirk is barely visible under his burly red beard, but his eyes dance with mischief. "Jormungundr, of course."

Beowulf runs to the ship. "I'm coming."

Thor chortles. "I wouldn't expect anything else." Thor reaches down to help him up, calling back to me at the same time, "Don't worry! I've got my belt and hammer. Everything is under control."

I place a hand on Elan's shoulder and lean against her side. "Yeah, I've heard that before," I say sarcastically.

- Chapter Nine -

As I watch them float farther out to sea, I call to Thor. "What are you going to use for bait?"

Thor holds up a decapitated head of a cow. "I harvested this off one of Hymir's favorite cows just before we came."

I screw up my nose and say the opposite of what I mean. "Lovely."

He threads it onto the end of a long line tied to the ship and throws it over the edge into the water. Directed by Beowulf, they sail out to the spot where we encountered the Midgard Serpent. The water is still. Not one ripple rises from under the surface.

Remaining on the water's edge, I press my tongue to the roof of my mouth. I hope I haven't scared the serpent away by shooting it with my magic. I analyze the still water, hoping for some sign of the monster. My spirits lift when the water ripples slightly only to be crushed when I realize it was caused by a large gust of wind.

My nerves are firing, the sparks intensifying with each uneventful moment. It's best if Thor captures the serpent now rather than wait until it becomes any bigger. Worried, I climb on Elan's back, dig through the pack attached to the saddle, and pull out my dragon-scale cloak. The sun glistens off the golden cloak made from the shed scales of Elan's family. I thread my arms through the cloak's sleeves, covering my quiver and sword slung on my back, and pull the hood over my head. I take special care to cover my legs and every part of the saddle. It's a ritual I have practiced many times. Not long after I made the gown, I learned that if the scales of the cloak are touching Elan's scales when she turns invisible, then the cloak and everything underneath its protection also turns invisible.

Once confident that I am covered, I gaze out over the ocean, searching for any sign of Jormungundr without success. "Perhaps we should do this while we're invisible. Maybe the monster will rise if it can't see us. It might be hiding after receiving a bolt of my magic."

Elan's scales disappear from underneath me along with every part that is covered by my golden-scaled cloak, leaving me with the sight of my hands grasping the straps attached to the saddle. Elan projects into the air, taking us higher with each flap of her enormous wings. The sensation of floating in midair fills me. It's a feeling that took time to become accustomed to. Every time she goes invisible beneath me, it's almost like I am the one flying, without the expelled energy.

Elan circles the area, the ground she's covered growing wider as the search proves fruitless. Eventually, a ripple rises from the depths of the ocean about a mile from the ship. My hopes rise again when I hover over the spot, and I'm rewarded with a glimpse of scales.

Elan tilts to the side and circles the area. *Did you see that?*

"Yes."

Without further instruction, Elan flies to the ship and hovers over Thor.

"It's not far away, Thor. It's still here," I call down to Thor, smiling to myself when he searches unsuccessfully for me. "But at the moment, it's lying low, probably because I shot it with magic not long before you arrived."

He scowls. "You did what?"

"I didn't have much choice. It was going to eat Elan and me."

"You know I would have saved you," Thor says, grinning toward the sound of my voice.

"That's not something I was willing to bet on. You'll find it about a mile northeast." I pull on the straps attached to Elan's neck. "Come on, Elan. Let's join the others."

Her body flips, and we fly back to land next to the other three dragons and my friends.

Elan turns visible, catching Hildr's attention immediately.

"What's going on?" Hildr asks.

"The serpent's lying low. I think I scared it off when I shot it with magic. It hasn't gone too far. We'll have to stand by in case Thor needs our help."

Britta groans. "I wish it would hurry up. I hate fishing. It's such a time waster."

I climb off Elan's back and lean against a tree, my eyes remaining fixed on the ocean. Something touches me on the shoulder, and I jump. Pushing the hood off my head and spinning, I find myself face-to-face with the red squirrel. Ratatoskr leans up against the trunk, his arms crossed and one leg hooked over the other, a smug look on his face.

"Ratatoskr! What are you doing here?"

He dusts his claws on his furry white chest, looks at them, then picks something out of his teeth. "Since you're on my radar now, I have a message to deliver."

"Oh. What is it?"

"Loki says you're a treacherous, grounded Valkyrie and you deserve the lot life has delivered you. He's disappointed in you. After giving you powers, all you did was use them against him."

I gasp. "What? He's the one who attacked Asgard." My voice is shrill.

The squirrel shrugs. "Hey, don't yell at me. I'm just the messenger." He scurries up the tree.

I scream at the squirrel while thumping the tree trunk. "Come back here, you little rat! I'll give you a message to deliver to that conniving Loki."

The tree stops shaking, and Ratatoskr pauses on one of the branches. He gazes down, his head tilting to the side, his expression curious. "And what would that be?"

I thought for a minute then yelled, "Loki is the treacherous being! He is the one who acted like my friend and betrayed me in all different forms." I cross my arms. "Pass that on to him."

Ratatoskr's furry brow bunches, and he crosses his arms, glaring down at me. He shakes his head. "That's not a good enough message to pass on to Loki. It has to be a better insult than what he called you."

My mind whirls. I'm not used to thinking of insults, yet after what he did, there's so much I want to say to Loki and haven't had the chance. "You tell Loki if he's so crafty and smart, then how did he father illegitimate children that turned into monsters? If he was clever, he wouldn't have had them in the first place."

The squirrel briefly screws up his tiny face then shrugs. "I guess that'll do. It's not the best one I've heard." He scurries up the branches, ignoring my astonished openmouthed glare as he disappears.

Elan nudges me from behind. *Are you okay?*

"What mess has Thor gotten me into? He has made me initiate contact with a squirrel that won't pass on messages unless it's insulting. Just what I don't need." I shake my head. "I thought I was finished with the mess Loki created. Now I'm dealing with his children, and not only that. He's haunting me from the depths of the cave he's tied up in."

Elan shows off her teeth in a gesture I have learned is a smile, although it's somewhat intimidating. *Would you like me to eat the squirrel next time it comes down?*

The thought brings a smile to my face, yet I shake my head and place a palm on the trunk of the tree. "As much as I like that idea, I think it's probably best not to. I think this terrible little squirrel has some oddly important role in Asgard and at the world tree."

The tree shakes, and the ground around it vibrates.

Elan's eyes widen. *What was that?* She cranes her massive head to try to get a better look as she stares up the tree.

"Ratatoskr probably just passed on an insulting message from the eagle to the dragon. He seems to take pleasure in annoying people. He told me when he tells the dragon, Nidhogg, something insulting from the eagle, the dragon gnaws at the roots of the world tree, trying to knock the eagle off Yggdrasil's top branches."

"Is the squirrel trying to kill the world tree? Doesn't he know that we need it to thrive in order to survive?" Eir interrupts our conversation.

I frown. "I wouldn't think Ratatoskr would want to kill the tree. He seems to love it."

The tree and ground shake some more, followed by a splash.

"What's going on?" Britta asks.

I gaze out to the ocean, noticing a swell growing in the water. "The rumbling of the ground and the shaking of the tree must be aggravating Jormungundr."

The murky-colored scales on the serpent's head

rise briefly out of the water as it thrashes some more. The boat drags forward, and Thor stands to check his line and see if the serpent is attached. His shoulders slouch when he realizes his rope is slack. Nothing has happened. Disappointment covers his face, then the rope in his hand tightens. Suddenly the boat pulls in the opposite direction, the rope attached to the cow's head going taut. The nose of the ship tilts toward the ocean before leveling then tilts again and rocks from bow to stern several times.

Beowulf and Hymir stand beside Thor, watching the line. Hymir's face blanches as the ship is dragged across the water. Thor straps on his belt for strength and grabs ahold of the rope.

Chapter Ten

The serpent dives and swishes so hard it drags the Viking ship several feet. Donning his metal gloves, Thor pulls on the rope, drawing the serpent above the water. Jormungundr opens its mouth, ready to swallow the bow of the ship.

Elan calls, *Jump on!*

Without a second thought, I swing onto her back, and she launches into the sky. I yank my sword out of its sheath then pull my hood on and close the edges of my dragon-scale cloak as we turn invisible.

With its mouth wide, the serpent rises higher, drawing the ship toward its mouth. Thor pulls on the rope as though reeling in a fish. I'm not sure what he's thinking. Between his pulling and the serpent's yanking, the ship is being sucked right into its open mouth. Thor's efforts might have been a good idea if the Midgard Serpent weren't trying to eat them.

I fling my sword at Jormungundr, lodging it deep in the flesh on the serpent's nose. The serpent cries, jams its mouth shut, and thrashes, the movement pulling the ship lower in the water. The waves splash up the sides and onto the deck.

Thor grabs Mjollnir and tosses his hammer directly at my sword, knocking it farther into the serpent. The monster cries again, flinging its head away from the ship and filling it with more water. Thor holds out his hand, calling to his hammer until it flies straight into his grasp.

The ship rocks and sways with the waves created by the serpent. Hymir frantically scoops buckets of water off the deck, tossing them back into the ocean to no avail. Jormungundr's frantic thrashing grows, pushing the sea up onto the land, exposing a section of the ocean floor.

The ship snags on the waterless ground, and Beowulf jumps over the edge and grasps ahold of the rope. This only makes the monster more agitated, and the thrashing increases. The water subsides more, and I notice that the walls of water are holding. Puzzled, I look up to see Britta, Hildr, and Eir sitting on their dragons and holding their palms out as though they are retaining the water with a massive wall of magic.

The bottom of the ocean is bare. Beowulf seems to notice what the Valkyries are doing, and he releases the rope, scoops up his spear, climbs a nearby boulder, and launches himself onto the serpent's back. His leather-strapped shoes slip on the scales, and his arms fling to the side, his spear held horizontally, until he regains his balance. The Midgardian runs along the serpent's back and onto its head.

Sensing something foreign on its back, the serpent lashes out some more. Nimbly, Beowulf runs to its head and slams the spear between its eyes then slides off its side. The rope tied to the ship yanks, pulling the ship closer to the serpent, dragging it along the dry seabed. Thor's body launches from the force.

I notice the giant is missing then spot Hymir crouching in the back of the ship, his face pale and his eyes wide. He pushes himself back onto his feet, trying to back farther into the corner and into the false sense of safety. I huff. It goes to show that bigger doesn't mean tougher. This is a perfect example.

As the serpent continues to slash, I call to my sword. The tiny wings on the hilt flap rapidly, trying to dislodge the blade from the monster's nose. I coax it some more, and at the same time, I gather my magic, letting it build, storing it in my necklace for another emergency.

An arrow shoots past me, careening directly at Jormungundr's eye. The serpent wriggles, and the arrow narrowly misses its target. I turn to see a bow in Britta's hand before she tucks it aside to hold out her hand to reinforce the wall of water.

With Hildr on his back, Drogon nose-dives straight toward the serpent. I grit my teeth. This maneuver could go wrong at any second, and I worry for Hildr. Suddenly, Drogon flips upside down, and Hildr points her sword at the serpent. A bolt of something shoots past her head as she flies forward.

Something crashes into the serpent, and within moments, the serpent halts its slashing and flops to the ground, unmoving. I glance up. Eir's hands are pointed in the direction of the serpent. She must have placed a stunning spell on it and is struggling to hold it.

Suddenly Britta yells, "Eir, work with me!" I realize that Britta has been left holding the walls of water, and they are crumbling at the sides, water breaking through the edges.

Eir glances at Hildr, who's almost at her target, then glances at the crumbling wall, assessing which is more urgent. Eir drops her stunning spell and helps Britta contain the water before Hildr can strike the serpent with her sword. The two Valkyries hover on their dragons, backs to each other, pressing their palms out to the water, holding it in place.

The serpent rears, pulling the ship closer. Drogon and Hildr swerve away from the attack, and Thor jumps down to Beowulf's side, lifting him onto the serpent's back to retrieve his spear. Thor tries to climb onto the serpent but slips to the ground when his feet can't find enough grip.

Giving up, Thor approaches the front of the monster, hammer in hand. Jormungundr snaps at him, black venom dripping from its fangs. I cringe when it snaps at him again, barely missing him. Beowulf slides off the serpent's back, giving up the pursuit of his spear.

Still invisible, I ride Elan, and she flips, granting me access to the spear's shaft sticking out of the serpent's head. I reach for it as we fly over but only manage to loosen it slightly. I groan as I'm unsuccessful in retrieving it from the serpent's flesh.

As Thor holds his hammer high, his face turns blank, his eyes unfocused as he stands fixed to the spot. Moments pass before thunder rumbles through the sky above. Eventually, lightning shoots across the sky several times before forking to the cleared ocean floor.

The walls of water cave slightly, and I fear anyone nearby will be electrocuted by lightning if the water reaches the strike spot.

Hildr joins Britta and Eir in holding the water walls with their magic, all three faces lost in concentration.

Britta groans. "I don't know how much longer I can hold this."

Giving up on my sword and the spear, I line up next to Eir, helping her with her wall of water while Hildr turns her full attention to Britta's side.

Displeased yells and groans reach our ears along with hisses from Jormungundr as it continues to inch its way toward the boat.

Thor stands again with Mjollnir held high, calling to the thunder and lightning. It rumbles and crackles, and light bolts across the sky. I sneak a peek. This is a sight that will never grow old. A bolt of lightning shoots down, hitting the hammer in Thor's hands, shoots up to the sky, then zaps the serpent close to its tail. After expelling a cry, the serpent thrashes some more.

Thor calls to the lightning again, this time using its force to lift him into the air, the hammer acting like a hot-air balloon. Suddenly, he thrusts the hammer at the serpent's head. His body drops as the hammer slams straight into the spear, embedding the shaft deeper into the serpent's flesh. The serpent's eyes widen with the impact, and it yanks itself backward, dragging the ship and the king of giants closer to its mouth.

When the serpent stops thrashing, it lowers its head to the ground until it realizes it isn't far away from the ship. Exposing its dripping fangs, it hisses. Hymir, crouched in the back of the boat, turns ghostly white, almost becoming a pale shade of blue as the serpent pulls him closer again.

I'm amazed that Jormungundr is still thrashing. The only answer I can think of is that the spear must have missed a vital spot.

Thor catches his hammer on its rebound then calls to the sky, releasing another bolt of lightning, hitting the serpent on the head. The muscles in the serpent's body tense before the serpent lashes to the side, striking Thor in the movement.

The god of thunder is tossed to the side and crashes against the side of the ship with a thud. Thor moans, and he takes a while to gather the energy to move, settling for a slow crawl.

Frantic thoughts whirl through my head as I assess the next best move. The serpent slithers forward, thankfully slowed by its massive form. On the ship, Hymir trudges forward, dagger in hand, his face still pale white. He reaches the bow, and shakily he saws the blade across the rope's fibers. The serpent lunges forward, rocking the ship, and the giant almost drops his dagger. Jormungundr yanks its head backward, dragging the attached boat closer until the final strokes of the dagger slice completely through the fibers, dropping the ship's hull to the ground.

Hildr cries, "Beowulf, grab Thor, and get out of there! We can't hold this much longer."

I feel the drain on my energy from exerting so much magic, but I was the last one to join them. It's then that I notice each of my friends' faces are covered in sweat.

Thor's face clouds with anger as he glowers in Hymir's direction. He grabs his hammer and dodges the serpent's snapping jaws as he and Beowulf charge to the ship and help each other onto the deck.

Thor stomps toward Hymir, his feet thumping on the wooden deck, his face full of anger and his hammer held high as he directs his failure to capture the serpent toward the giant.

Slowly, the Valkyries release the walls of water, lifting the boat up evenly and submersing Jormungundr's body. The monster lashes out at the ship one last time.

Noticing that Thor is too distracted by his anger

toward the king of giants to see the threat from the serpent, Beowulf grabs Hymir's discarded dagger from the ship's deck and tosses it blade-first into the monster's mouth. The point lodges in its tongue. Jormungundr rears back and circles away from the boat.

Chapter Eleven

Thor stomps toward Hymir, his hammer held high and his face fuming. "We're supposed to stop the serpent, not let it go. You know the prediction. It could cause Ragnarok and be the end of Asgard."

Hymir's face remains pale, and despite his size, he cowers from Thor's raised hammer. "I wasn't about to become the serpent's meal."

Thor scowls, his eyes barely visible under his bushy red eyebrows. He throws the hammer into the water in the serpent's direction then waits, with his hand outstretched, for its return. "It's not about one being or god. It's about the whole of Asgard and stopping anything that may cause Ragnarok."

Mjollnir launches out of the water, and with a wave of his hand, Thor directs the hammer at Hymir. It hits the giant in the stomach, knocking him overboard. Instantly, the hammer returns to Thor's outstretched hand, leaving the giant struggling in the ocean. Ignoring Hymir's cry for help, Thor steers the Viking ship back to shore.

"Elan, turn visible, please," I say.

She obliges, and we fly down to level with Thor.

"You can't just leave him there." I gaze past the ship to see Hymir splashing awkwardly in the background, trying to swim and sinking fast.

Thor growls and places his hammer on the ground. "And what good is he back home? He let the serpent go."

I spread my hands out to my sides. "He was scared. Everybody gets scared sometimes, despite our size and abilities. Clearly, his size doesn't amount to his courage. I get that you're annoyed with him, but don't just leave him in the deep water. We'll have another go at catching the serpent later."

Thor crosses his arms over his chest. "I'm not turning around."

Elan flaps her wings with a mighty whoosh, showing her displeasure and blowing Thor's bushy red hair in a minitornado.

My mouth gapes in disbelief. This a side of Thor I haven't seen before, not that I've been in battle with him until now. I already know I don't like this side. "Don't you think your warriors will worry that you will leave them in battle if they get scared?"

Thor lifts his chin. "We choose the bravest of warriors from Midgard. They won't do that." He gestures to the Midgard beast slayer. "Just look at Beowulf. He didn't cower."

"He specializes in destroying monsters. Others from Midgard might get scared, depending on what they have to face in battle. Not all warriors can stand up against the beasts. Beowulf is an exception." I click my tongue against the roof of my mouth. "Look. I know you're angry right now, but you can't leave him stranded."

Thor huffs loudly. "If you want to get him, go get him. I won't stop you."

I thought Thor would give in eventually, which is why I persisted. He's usually one of the more under-standing gods, but now I'm in a dilemma. "And how do you expect me to carry him? Elan is strong but not strong enough to carry a giant plus me."

Hildr and Drogon line up next to me. "We'll help you."

I gaze at Drogon, and he nods once, tilting the horns on his head forward. His brown form is smaller than Elan's, although more robust than the other two dragons'.

Elan rises, heading in Hymir's direction. The giant is barely visible on the wavy surface of the ocean. His head disappears underwater for a moment before breaking the surface and sucking in an exasperated breath. His arms fly and flop in all directions, clearly indicating that the giant can't swim. Dull-colored serpent scales skim the water's surface behind the giant, bringing with them all kinds of dangerous scenarios. I clamp my teeth shut and swallow the lump in my throat. I hope we get to him before the serpent decides to eat him.

Elan's strong wings carry us to him with several strokes, and Drogon follows closely behind. She swoops down and grabs the giant's hands, and I can feel her struggle with the added weight as she drags him higher. Drogon catches hold of Hymir's feet as Elan pulls him out of the water. Together they carry him away from the sea, his massive form swinging uncomfortably between them.

Elan grunts, a sound indicating she is struggling with the weight. *I'm so glad you're helping, Drogon. I couldn't do this on my own.*

Their flight wavers, and they drop toward the ocean, barely missing Thor's ship. My heart jumps to my throat.

Naga flies next to us. *Let Naga help. Kara, hop on Naga's back. It will lighten Elan's load.*

"Good thinking, Naga!" I call.

With Eir on his back, Naga swoops down below me just underneath Hymir's arms. I jump, the air catching my dragon-scale cloak, causing it to billow and flap. I spread my legs, trying to straddle Naga. My backside thumps onto Naga's back, and his flight path dips and swerves as we careen toward the water, skimming its surface. Eir embraces me, stopping my fall as my body tilts to the side. Naga's wings pump as he labors to carry us higher, away from the ocean and to the shore.

That helped heaps, Naga. Thank you. Elan already sounds less strained.

Tanda circles around us and catches Hildr, lightening Drogon's load. Hildr slips on Tanda's mound, which looks similar to that of a one-humped camel, her body built differently than the other dragons, and she falls toward the red dragon's tail. Tanda extends her tail and tightens the muscles along its length, trying to support the wingless Valkyrie before she falls. Hildr quickly reaches for Britta's hand. The strain on the Valkyrie's arms is evident in her flexed muscles as Britta clasps her strap with one arm and Hildr with the other. Hildr yanks and claws her way to the edge of Tanda's one-person saddle shaped to fit her hump and wraps her hands around Britta's waist. Thankfully there is only a short distance to the shore to relieve the pressure on the dragons and Hildr's grasp.

Naga lands, followed shortly by Tanda. Elan and

Drogon gently set the soaked Hymir down and land with a thud not far from the other dragons, their breathing heavy from the weight of the giant. They tuck their wings close to their sides.

By the time the ship sails to the shore, the dragons are recovered, and Hymir slowly stands. Thor jumps out of the ship, Beowulf not far behind him, helping Thor drag the boat to the shore. Thor folds the ship up and places it in his bag, a feat I don't know why I struggle to believe. After all, the Asgardians get mead out of a goat.

With brooding faces, Thor and Beowulf approach us, their warrior's chests broad and their muscular arms swinging by their sides.

Hymir blocks Thor's path, his giant body rigid with tension. "I'm so sorry. I got scared. It's stupid, I know. I acknowledge I'm not worth more than Asgard's future. I came because I thought I'd be helpful, but instead, I was a hindrance." He looks at the ground, dejected and sad.

Deep lines crease Thor's forehead as he approaches the massive form. At first, I'm not sure whether or not Thor is going to punch him until the god places a hand on Hymir's arm. "I understand. I'm sorry I threw you in the water. I let my anger get the better of me. But next time, stay away."

Thor leaves the baffled giant and approaches his

carriage, rubbing one of the goats that pulls it behind the ear as he passes. He waves to Beowulf. "Until next time." After climbing onto the carriage, he grabs the straps and appears as though he is about to leave without the giant.

A moment passes before he calls over his shoulder, "Are you coming, Hymir?"

Without a word, the giant runs toward the carriage and sits next to Thor, his face still bearing the signs of regret and disappointment.

As they leave, I turn to Beowulf. "Are you seriously the one who slays the monsters on Midgard?"

"True to my word." He pushes out his chest proudly.

"The next time you see Jormungundr, can you send word to us so we can try to defeat it together?"

"And how am I supposed to do that?"

I stare at him in disbelief. "Haven't you sent word to Thor before?"

"No. We always just run into each other when he's on Midgard in the middle of a battle and I'm tackling some monster."

I gaze at the still waters of the ocean, my mind whirling. I can see only one solution, and I'm not that fond of it, but it may work. "Have you met Ratatoskr?"

He looks confused. "Who is that?"

"It's a squirrel that lives in Yggdrasil, the world tree."

The creases in his brow deepen. "I've seen lots of squirrels. What are you talking about?"

"I don't mean squirrels of Midgard. I mean the squirrel that runs up and down the world tree carrying messages."

He shakes his head. "No."

I let out a long breath. "Okay. I'll show you where to call him. I only met the squirrel today, but he's a very feisty little thing." I approach the world tree branches where I met Ratatoskr earlier. "Here goes." I raise my voice and call up the tree. "Ratatoskr!"

Within moments, I hear scurrying, and his little red face peers out of a hole in the tree. The squirrel's nose twitches, and his beady eyes fall on Beowulf.

"Ratatoskr, this is Beowulf. If he calls you, can you come?"

The squirrel's eyes narrow, and he screws up his nose as he stands straight on his two back feet. His tail flicks from side to side. "What am I, a servant?"

"I know you're not a servant. However, we need someone who can carry a message from Midgard to Asgard, and you are the messenger of the world tree."

The squirrel huffs, crossing his arms over his chest as he narrows his gaze on Beowulf.

"If Beowulf needs to get a message to Thor or to me, can you please come down when he calls you?" I plead.

Ratatoskr runs down the tree and up Beowulf's body. The warrior cringes with each scratch the cheeky messenger leaves on his skin. The squirrel scrambles around his shoulders, flexing and pulling on the warrior's bulging muscles in his arms and torso before drawing back and staring straight into Beowulf's eyes.

"I guess he is a fine specimen for a Midgardian." Ratatoskr turns to me. "Have you told him about my conditions?"

"No, I haven't. I wasn't sure if that was something you asked of everyone or just me."

The squirrel tuts then faces Beowulf. "I only carry messages that are insults." He then scurries down Beowulf and up Yggdrasil before disappearing into the hole.

"That's an interesting little creature." Beowulf's eyes are fixed on the hole Ratatoskr disappeared into, and he looks confused.

With raised eyebrows, I nod. "You don't have to tell me!"

Chapter Twelve

We ride into Asgard and separate, going our different ways. I have a sudden urge to visit Odin and see if he's okay. It seems like a long time since I saw him that night outside the entrance of Yggdrasil leading to Mimir's well. The thought has me chuckling. It was only a couple of years ago that I would never have considered visiting Odin of my own free will. But he's changed since the colossal attack on Asgard. I guess some of his stubbornness broke that day.

An image of a crumpled Odin flashes in my mind, reminding me that something broke him this time as well and not in a good way.

After leaving Elan in the large courtyard at the side of the palace, I skim the steps, taking them two at a time. Both sides of the entrance are manned by two guards.

"Greetings, Valkyrie!" the guard on the left calls.

His small chin barely holds the strap of his helmet and contrasts with his large, pointy nose, making his normal-sized eyes seem small in comparison.

"Greetings, Birger!" I call before reaching the top of the steps.

His face spreads into a broad smile.

"Greetings, Gorm!" I call to the guard on the right.

A glimmer of appreciation passes through the eyes of the guard with the large chin divided by a cleft. "Who are you coming to see today?"

It was only a couple of years ago that they would do anything to stop me from getting inside the palace. How times have changed. "I've come to visit Odin. Is he here?"

"We haven't seen him leave," Gorm says.

They open the doors to the palace, indicating for me to go through. I enter the large, open corridors lined with marble and massive pillars. The extravagance is impressive and far from the state of my residence and the Valkyrie Academy. My shoes scuff loudly on the floor from my open and unafraid steps.

So many times in the past, I had to hide when I passed through these halls. It's a nice change, not having to hide behind every pillar to avoid the guards as I weave through the palace.

A guard stands outside the throne room, and I

enter through the double doors unhindered only to find it empty.

I exit, bearing a frown of confusion as I glance at the guard outside in the hall.

His spine is rigid and tall as it presses toward the wall. His horned helmet overwhelms his head, and his curious blue eyes meet mine as he gazes down at me. "Greetings, Kara. Why are you here?"

"I've come to see Odin."

"He is unwell. He hasn't been to the throne room today."

I push my mouth to the side in thought. "Yes, I heard. I've come to see how he is and update him on some news."

The guard nods once. "I will escort you to his chambers and see if he wants to see you."

"Thank you, Den."

It was only a couple of years ago that Den was dragging me back to the Valkyrie Academy, far away from Odin.

He clicks his heels together and nods once, then marches down the hallway, his sword swinging by his side, the hilt clanking against his armor. I follow him until we reach another set of large, decoratively carved, wooden double doors.

Den stops and speaks over his shoulder. "Wait here. I'll check if he wants to see you."

Before I can answer, he yanks on the sizeable golden handle and pushes into the room, shutting the doors behind him. Muffled voices, too soft to decipher, seep through the thick wood.

The golden handle jolts down, and the door cracks open. Den's face peers through the space. "Odin says he'll see you."

He pulls the door open, and I slip past the guard. Ample burgundy folds of material drape from the canopy over Odin's massive king-size bed. The god is lying on a mattress that appears to be several layers thick, his back propped up by an extravagant number of cushions.

With my eyes fixed on Odin's pale face, my boot catches on something. I glance down and gasp. The top of my boot is stuck under an uplifted scale of a golden dragonhide spread across the floor like a decorative mat.

"Oh. Don't mind that. It was my father's." Odin sounds apologetic. "It's centuries old. I haven't had it removed yet. To be honest, I'm not in my room often."

I glance up at the pale-faced god almost swallowed in cushions and buried in blankets. He looks so frail compared to a few days ago. A haunted eye gazes at me, and for now, I push aside my disgust over the dragonhide. I unhook my boot from the scale and sidestep the floor decoration as I approach him, noticing his staff propped against the wall next to his bed.

"Kara, thank you for visiting." The god's voice is husky, a shadow of its former strength.

"I had to see how you were, great Odin."

I move closer to his bed, taking in his hollow cheeks and the dark ring around his eye not hidden behind the patch. Odin pats the side, indicating for me to sit. I do as instructed, feeling out of place sitting on the god's bed. Even though he isn't himself, his eye doesn't shift, making me uneasy even with his weakened state.

"I'm sorry you had to see that the other night."

I push away my discomfort. "Great Odin, everybody has their moments of weakness. I won't let it spread that you had one too."

A massive sigh of relief pushes out of his lungs. "Thank you. I appreciate it. If others on Asgard hear about my..." He pauses, his expression pained. "Weakness, it may cause unrest and anxiety."

I place a hand on his bed, closer to his body, wanting to add comfort but not wanting to touch the god without permission. "That is why I have kept it to myself, and I'm sure Eingana will do the same. I believe it's important to keep this quiet. Asgard doesn't need to worry about its leader falling apart."

"That's very wise, young Valkyrie. Some might not be able to handle knowing their leader has a meltdown occasionally."

"I understand."

I jump as the door suddenly crashes open against the wall and Thor's large form enters, his eyes wild and face burning with concern and worry. "Forgive me, Father. I have failed."

Odin's brow creases in a frown, his eyes falling to me as though looking for answers.

"As I promised, I told Thor about what you said about Loki's three children from his giant mistress and how they need to be contained."

Odin nods. "That was a wise move." He turns to Thor, gesturing to the chair next to his bed. "Sit."

Without a moment wasted, Odin's ginger-haired son obeys.

Odin's dull gaze assesses Thor. "How have you failed?"

Thor throws his head in his hands and rests his elbows on his knees as he stares at his lap. "I took Hymir the giant to help me catch Jormungundr, thinking his size would be of help. Except Hymir buckled in fear and cut the rope when I nearly had the serpent."

Odin nods. "Ah, yes. It was foretold that would be so," he says in a calm voice.

Thor glances up from his lap, his eyes boring into Odin. "And is it foretold that we will catch Jormungundr before it wreaks havoc?"

"No. It is foretold that the Midgard Serpent will be part of Ragnarok and will be part of Asgard's downfall as well as your own." Odin holds up a finger. "But prophecies aren't set in stone. They can be changed if we take a different path from how it was foretold."

"I hope you're right because not even Beowulf is willing to tackle the serpent by himself. It has grown so big. If it gets any bigger, it will be much harder to handle. A simple fishing line or rope will not withstand its weight."

"I understand," Odin says. "What about Fenrir? Did you manage to contain him?"

"No. We didn't," Thor says. "We tried. We chained him with the chains that we used on the dragons, but he broke out within minutes. He is so strong."

Odin nods. "Yes, that was also foretold, but we must not panic."

"He still seems mostly the same, a happy pup." Thor's shoulders soften as some of the stress leaves his body. "But if the prophecy says he is dangerous, then we should take measures." Thor's gaze lands on me momentarily before he continues. "There haves been some reports that he has moments of aggression. We will keep working on restraining him."

Odin nods once. "And Hel?"

"I haven't seen any evidence that Hel is on the rise. I will leave her alone for the moment and try to settle these two—unless something changes."

Odin's face looks distant and slightly scared before he responds. "I believe Fenrir is our most significant risk at the moment. I know it is hard to believe, but try to contain him soon. I can see his anger burning."

Chapter Thirteen

Thor and I leave Odin's room and exit the palace.

"I'm going to find out how the gods and forgers are going making a stronger chain for Fenrir. You can come if you like. Otherwise, you're relieved of your duties. You've worked hard today."

A memory of Fenrir as a pup flashes into my mind. He was so adorable, his fur soft and his nature loving. It's hard to believe he's changing into something dangerous. Deep anguish churns in my stomach. I shake my head. "I think I'll sit this one out and have some time by myself, or with Elan. I don't like thinking of Fenrir as something dangerous, and it upsets me seeing living creatures chained when they haven't done anything wrong."

Thor's blue eyes survey me. "You didn't seem to mind with the Midgard Serpent."

"Yes, but Jormungundr was a monster from the start. Fenrir used to be a cute, loving pup."

Thor yanks on the base of his tunic and wriggles as though making it more comfortable. "I understand. I'll see you later." He leaves me, heading in the direction of where the gods train for battle and the place Fenrir will likely be sleeping by Tyr's side.

I make my way to the courtyard, where I left Elan next to the palace. When I round the corner to the courtyard, she is nowhere to be found. I halt then spin to search the area only to see Birger standing by the palace door, a broad smile plastered across his face.

I follow his line of sight to find Gorm walking with exaggerated steps, a look of excitement on his face as he throws handfuls of dirt. I watch him do this a few more times. He halts twice, his body rigid and his eyes on full alert.

I call to Birger, "What is he do—"

A shocked yell comes from Gorm, and when I look, his body is floating, and laughter explodes from his mouth. I raise an eyebrow as Elan becomes visible with Gorm clasped in her talons, and she gently lowers him to the ground.

We're playing hide and seek. Elan's voice answers my unfinished question.

"I see." I smile and shake my head. My dragon is like a big kid, and she has found some playmates. I would never have envisioned this a couple of years ago when Gorm and Birger were making my life difficult.

"Come, Elan. Stop playing with the grown man."

With a look of disappointment, Elan sinks to the ground, making it easier for me to climb onto her saddle. I grab the reins and stroke her shoulder. "I can't believe you're supposed to rule the dragons one day. You're the biggest child of them all."

What's life without a bit of fun? She exposes her teeth in what is supposed to be a smile. "That's where you can rule your herd in a completely different way than your mother."

She pushes off, flapping her enormous wings. The breeze pushes the dirt into clouds, and pebbles scatter noisily across the courtyard floor. We rise above the palace, and Elan asks, *Where to?*

The rocky mountains of Asgard spread out before us. I rub my tongue behind my top teeth. "I think I'd like to see the old cave, the one where Gilroma used to stay. Well, Loki."

Really? Elan doesn't hide the shock in her voice.

"Ah, huh. My magic hasn't grown since he's been locked up. There's no one to teach me." Absentmindedly, I clasp the blue-stone necklace around my neck. Slight nostalgia courses through my veins. "To be honest, I miss those days. I still find it hard to believe he's completely evil and working for the opposite side."

I drop the necklace, and my brows pinch together as Elan veers toward the mountain.

"I don't understand why he stole the dragon eggs to raise an army and why he did what he did, but I do miss the education he gave me."

When we reach the mountain, she circles and lands outside the long tunnel.

I gaze into the darkness, rawly aware of the lack of light in the passage I'm about to enter. "Elan, can you please breathe fire on the linked torches on either side of the wall?"

Elan chuckles. *It does look a little spooky down there.*

She stretches her neck and expels a controlled flame from her mouth, igniting the first torch in line. The fire follows the oil path to the next sconce, lights it, then continues past the extent of my vision. She does the same to the other side.

Musty, stale air assaults my nostrils as I follow the long tunnel down the center of the mountain, and eerie sounds echo off the enclosed walls. I had forgotten the hair-raising feeling I felt the first time I discovered the tunnel. The sensation dimmed in the trips afterward, when I knew I had Gilroma to call on if something went wrong. He was nearly always down at the other end, hiding in his cave.

I haven't been here for quite some time, probably before the last attack on Asgard, when I thought this was a friend's cave. I shake the thought from my head. If the sentence given to Loki is accurate, I was mistaken. Still, even if he's guilty, I'm sure there's valuable information in the books he was hoarding here.

The wind blows from behind me, bringing fresh air and something else. I breathe deeply, trying to work out if it's an odd smell on the breeze, and I come up with nothing. Even so, a strange feeling brushes my skin, giving me the sudden urge to look around. My search remains fruitless, and I push forward to the small rooms at the end, my eyes wide with anticipation as I round the corner. Eerie shadows creep along the stone walls. The flames of the sconces dance on the breeze, and a faintly rancid smell leaks from the burning oil. No one must have visited here after Loki was put away.

My footsteps warn the room I'm entering as I pace straight for the large pile of books neatly stacked in the corner. I run my fingers over the cover of the first book, leaving streaks in the dust. My leather pants creak as I plunk my backside on the stone bench, pulling the top book onto my lap and dusting the cover with my hand. The pages are illuminated by the light from the sconce over my shoulder.

My fingers tremble as I flick through the pages, excitement pulsing through them as they glide over the pages. Dark elves' magic is written in these pages, something I haven't touched for a long time. My magic is so limited, especially since Gilroma can no longer train me.

Yet, as I flick through the pages, my excitement diminishes. The book is written in the language of the dark elves, a language I can't understand let alone read. It looks as though I'm going to have to learn another language. I may have to go back to the library in the academy and see if they have any books on this.

Different elven symbols cover the pages with not one word in a language I understand. It is going to take an immense amount of time to learn this. With disappointment coursing through me, I close the book and set it aside before grabbing the next. Again the pages are filled with a language I don't understand. I work my way through each book in the pile until, finally, I toss the last book aside with a disappointed sigh. A substantial weight pushes on my shoulders.

Besides myself, I have three friends who can do magic, but we're almost entirely untrained. This needs to change. Even though we helped defeat the dark elves that invaded Asgard, there are still threats of another attack and perhaps Ragnarok. My brows pinch together, my mind deep in thought as I stare at each of the unique book covers.

Suddenly, Elan's voice pierces my thoughts. *Kara, wherever you are, don't come out. I hope you're way down in the middle of that mountain.*

My frown deepens. "Why do you say so, Elan?" I know her hearing is good and that she should be able to hear me, but she doesn't answer. With my curiosity piqued, I leave the cave and work my way down the long tunnel. When I'm about halfway, I ask again. "Why do you ask, Elan?"

You're louder. You better not be coming down the tunnel, Elan scolds.

"You didn't answer me before, so I was coming out to make sure you heard me."

Her voice rises, panic lacing the words. *You better not be coming down the tunnel. You better be doing what you're told you. Go back into the cave, Kara!*

The sound of rocks toppling and quick movements echo down the tunnel. I tilt my ear toward the entrance. If I'm not mistaken, there is scuffling just outside accompanied by a growl, deep and long. Shivers run down my spine. That didn't sound like Elan. I quicken my steps, pushing toward the entrance.

You better be retreating to the end of that cave, Kara. Those better not be your footsteps I hear approaching. If they are, I'll never let you live this down. I'll make you pay one way or another.

Suddenly her tail enters the tunnel, slashing as her body writhes. Her long golden tail swings from one side to the other, knocking anything in its wake.

"What are you doing, Elan? Are you fighting something out there?" I move as close to the edge of the tunnel as I can, avoiding her thrashing tail.

She stops wriggling, and I move closer to her as my eyes catch a spot I can slip through, only to jump back to dodge another swing. I wait, tethering my impatience, for a chance to go outside to help her. As though reading my mind, in a split second, she backs up, blocking the whole entrance with her backside. I hear another muffled, deep, and menacing growl.

I stomp my foot, frustrated over feeling helpless. "What is going on, Elan? Let me help you."

No, Kara. Stay where you are. This is not a fight you can help me with.

An ear-piercing scream splits the air, making my

heart skip a beat. Elan flicks her tail again, narrowly missing me. I edge my way up the tunnel even though it's still blocked by her backside.

"What is that? Let me help you, Elan."

No, Kara. Stay where you are. This is nothing from Asgard.

Chapter Fourteen

My interest piques. "What do you mean?"

Elan doesn't answer.

"What is it?"

A tremendous growl reaches my ears, and I press close to Elan's backside, trying to avoid her thrashing tail.

I screech, "Elan, let me out! I want to help you."

No. I told you to stay there.

A grunt travels through her mind speak, followed by a groan so filled with pain I almost think I'm the one who was struck.

"Elan, are you all right?"

She groans, this time with frustration. *You weren't meant to hear that.*

I stomp my foot. She's being overprotective. "Well, I did. So let me out to help you."

No.

Another moan travels through a small crack

between Elan's butt and the side of the tunnel. It isn't loud, as most of the sound is muffled, yet it still sets my nerves on edge. My hands curl into tight fists, my nails biting into the flesh of my palms. Something is attacking her, something big and powerful. Try as I might, I'm at a loss thinking of a creature that is bigger and stronger than a dragon Elan's size. I can't piece together what could be attacking her.

Growling followed by Elan's sudden movements of her backside only make my fear for my dragon rise. My heart pounds in concern for Elan facing whatever monster this is alone. More dragon cries seep into the tunnel and echo down its length, chilling me to the bone. I have to get out there.

A loud roar filled with pain bursts from an unfamiliar creature, and inwardly I cheer for Elan.

Suddenly, Elan jerks forward, and another unknown creature's roar follows. Elan's body lurches to the left, and a larger crack opens between her backside and the side of the tunnel. I contemplate running through the opening, yet I'm also aware that if Elan jerks quickly to the right, I could be squashed. I work up the courage only to have it crushed when suddenly she flings back, covering the gap. I badly want to get out and help her.

My heart pounds so rapidly that it thrums in my ears, making it harder to hear. Thankfully it blocks some of Elan's cries of pain. I'm ready to stick my head out of the new opening she has made, when suddenly Elan's hip slams to the right, her scales narrowly missing my face as she closes the gap. I jump back and try to escape her tail swinging in my direction.

"Elan. You've got to let me out."

No! She sounds as though she's hissing through clenched teeth.

I huff with disapproval. I've got to get out there somehow. She needs help whether she'll admit it or not.

Another dragon cry pierces the air, and she suddenly flings to the left again. In a split second, I run toward the crack, narrowly skimming past, only to have her slam to the right again just after I scrape my last limb through the opening.

My stomach lurches to my throat. That was close. Her foot suddenly flies in my direction, and I narrowly dodge it. Elan concentrates on the beast as she prepares to take it on again.

I move around the side of her, and I'm confronted with the face of a hideous beast. Fire seems to burn in its eye sockets. The creature opens its mouth, exposing flames within the depths of its throat. Unlike a dragon, it doesn't seem to have the ability to breathe plumes of fire. Instead, its insides appear to be made of molten lava that burns deep within its stomach to its very core. Each time it opens its mouth and eyes, they fill with the glowing red flames.

My jaw drops. I have no idea what this is. It's like nothing I've ever heard of before. Its body is black, and horns protrude from its skull, like a dragon, yet it has no wings.

I scan its shape, my eyes traveling up and up as I crane my neck to see its face. It's hideously tall, taller than Elan when it stands on its two legs, its long arms dangling from its sides. I haven't seen anything like this in the books I've read in the Valkyrie Academy library. If we survive this, I will have to revisit the unique monsters section to search for this beast.

Pushing aside my shock, I steel myself. I'm not going to let Elan fight this alone. I press my back against the rock wall of the mountain, strangely finding some comfort in the solid form at my back. The creature swings its arm, and long claws protrude from its fingerlike digits. It rakes its claws up Elan's side, striking against the flow of her scales, hooking into the soft flesh hidden deep beneath them.

My face twists as I imagine the agony she's experiencing. My horror deepens when she expels a pain-filled roar.

With an openmouthed stare, I ponder the best

way to tackle this. This beast is way too big for one Valkyrie and her loyal dragon. We thought the dark elves and frost giant that invaded Asgard earlier, threatening to bring on Ragnarok, were bad enough. I need to stop and assess the situation so I can work out how to tackle this massive monster. The only problem with thinking it through is it will use precious time I don't have. As much as I need to, I don't have the luxury of sitting back and assessing. I have to act now, or this will be the end of Elan and undoubtedly myself not long afterward. My feet shake in my boots as I think of what I might need to do. Even so, it's not the first time I've had to battle a monster.

The monster shifts one of its feet, drawing my attention. Its foot is almost the size of Elan's enormous head, its tall legs reaching halfway up her body if not higher. The legs lead to a long thin frame and spindly arms and a head that's bigger than Elan's. The mouth is similar to a wolf's. I shudder at the thought of what could happen if that mouth came anywhere near me. As I work hard to contain my fear, it dawns on me that the thing doesn't have wings.

Elan lurches forward, horns first, aiming straight for the creature's stomach. The beast's mouth opens wide as it lets out a roar, revealing its lava contents.

Elan twists and flicks her head, one horn ripping at the monster's torso. It throws its head back, releasing a cry of agony.

Elan pulls back then charges forward again, this time using the horns from both sides of her head. Quickly she flicks her head down, releasing her horns from the brute's body, showing off the two fiery holes that she dug.

The beast's arms flail wide before raking up Elan's back. Her screech cuts to my very core as the lava monster rakes its claws up her sides, stopping before it hits the saddle, narrowly missing Elan's wings. Blood trickles down Elan's sides.

I've watched enough horror befalling my beloved dragon. I must think of a way to help. I study her wings, my heart leaping with hope when I notice that they look intact. I have an idea, but I must get on Elan's back first, and I can't distract her from the fight. That might be fatal. I also know that she would be most upset with me if she realized that I was out of the protection of the tunnel and would probably knock me back into it and block me in there again. At least if I were already on her, it would be harder for her to entrap me in the tunnel. I have to get onto her back without her help.

Keeping an eye on the monster, I assess the area and the situation. I must dodge this massive beast and its swiping dark claws. Thankfully, Elan has been keeping it busy, and I don't think it has seen me yet.

Elan's tail remains pressed into the tunnel's entrance. She must think that I'm still trapped within its confines. Amusing as it is, it's also hindering her movements to defend herself. I must get on her back and let her know that I am safe so she can move away from the tunnel, giving her more freedom to flip and move.

On the mountainside, I spot a ledge and a rocky, jagged path that might be possible to climb. Quickly, I head to the rugged track, grasping the rocks on the cliff face and pulling myself up as hastily as I can. I lunge for a difficult spot, clasping a small ledge, only to lose traction. My hands, elbows, knees, and face scrape against the rough rocks before my hand manages to find purchase on a lower ledge. My arms and legs feel weak. My heart pounds in my chest as I tackle the fear of knowing I could have slid to my death. I peer between the rock face and my armpit, taking in the distance to the ground, confirming my suspicions. It's not too far but still far enough to injure me enough to be useless.

Controlling my breath, I focus on my mission and brace my emotions, toughening up. I yank myself upward, drawing my weight higher before hooking a leg over the ledge. I gaze over my shoulder to monitor the position of the beast. The glowing red eyes seem to be looking at me, but I'm not sure. They don't have any pupils, making it hard to know exactly where it's focusing. Quickly, I yank myself up and turn around to assess the situation from my new viewpoint.

The beast flings its arms in my direction. I'm not sure if it's aiming for Elan or me. Elan dodges the strike, and the claws swing over Elan and scrape along the rock wall at the height of my legs. I jump as high as I can, managing to avoid its hand. As though it hasn't spotted me, the monster continues to attack Elan, her backside still pressed against the tunnel. Maybe the swipe was always intended for Elan, and it just missed.

I study the height of Elan's back. It's still too high for me to jump on. I have to climb farther. I struggle up another level before facing the backside of my best friend and dragon, assessing the distance between us. I ready myself, moving my legs into a sturdy position, and lift my arms before leaping off the ledge. I fling my arms behind me to try to gather more speed before reaching forward and clasping onto the saddle on Elan's back.

She jumps, unaware of my position, and her wild golden eyes glance over her shoulder. *Kara, what on dragon's scales are you doing out of that tunnel? I told you to stay in there.*

"I can't let you fight this alone. You need my help, and you need to stop protecting that tunnel. It's hindering your fighting ability."

Her eyes narrow, the disapproval evident in her glare. Suddenly, something black flings in her direction.

All emotion drops from my face. "Look out, Elan!"

Chapter Fifteen

Elan whirls just in time to see the monster's claws careening toward her. They rake up her scales along her face, and she cries out in pain, the scream projecting into my mind. The weight of her distress weakens my limbs. She lurches back, and I manage to cling onto the straps just enough to stay on.

The sudden jerk awakens my purpose. "Elan! Use your wings! Push into the air!" I screech.

Elan swings sideways, away from being pinned to the tunnel, blood seeping from her scales.

With a groan of pain, she lurches forward two bounds before springing at the monster with her head down. Her horns ram straight into the creature's abdomen, knocking it backward as she pushes with all her might.

I groan. She ignored my advice.

The monster folds over the top of Elan and stares

down at me, shadowing me in blackness and molten lava. I grasp the power that's been welling inside of me, ready to help defend, and aim my hands directly at the creature's face. I'm not sure if this is going to do anything. This creature looks like a creature of magic. I cling to hope as my power hits it in the face.

The lava monster straightens and staggers backward, a strange look passing over its hideous features. The movement dislodges it from Elan's horns, and a shudder runs down her body. She groans in pain from the wounds all over her body, and lethargically, she pushes into the air.

Seeing Elan's progress seems to revive the creature from its setback. Regaining its strength, it shifts forward, its footsteps pounding on the ground. A long black arm reaches for Elan, claws extended.

At the last second, Elan swerves to fly away from the monster, narrowly avoiding the strike. The creature roars its frustration, sending shivers down my spine.

Elan peers over her shoulder, and I follow her line of sight, spotting the horrid black arm striking out again. Elan furls her wings, and we plummet just in time to dodge the strike. The wind from the attack blows on my face as the extended claws miss me by a foot. I retaliate by sending another bolt of magic at the creature's face, and it topples onto its backside.

Elan unfurls her wings, catching the breeze and carrying us from the monster's reach before it strikes again. She flies several more yards, no longer needing to dodge the monster's attacks. Now that the immediate threat is reduced, I notice her usually controlled flight seems to waver. I concentrate on her and fret. She seems to be struggling underneath me.

"Are you all right?"

Exhaustion and pain reverberate through the words that enter my head. *Not really.*

Worry fills my every pore. Her safety is paramount to me, yet there is a monster still lurking on Asgard. We can't stay and fight. Elan is in no condition to continue. I glance over my shoulder, finding the beast still on its backside, but it won't be for long. I don't know what to do. I can't call the others, and we don't need this thing causing any more havoc.

"Can you make it back?"

Maybe.

My heart sinks. Flying is still the quickest way back, and I can't do that for her. She needs help as soon as possible. I rub my hands together, focusing on my magic, then inject all the strength I can into her. Hopefully, it will help heal her, but I don't like our odds. She looks terrible.

We fly a little way, and I spot two forms in the air heading toward us.

"Who's approaching?" I ask, unable to see them in the distance.

The weariness in her voice shatters me. *It's Drogon and Tanda with Hildr and Britta. I called them when I was fighting... whatever it is. They are coming to assist me.*

I steel my emotions. "Thanks, great thinking, but I don't think two dragons are going to be enough to defeat that thing."

I told them as much, Elan says, sounding more exhausted with every word that projects into my head.

The distance between the two dragons and us closes, and I indicate for them to land. At least Elan can have a brief rest while I update the others. We circle down and land on a rocky plain.

I call to the others, "I don't think two dragons will be enough to fight that thing."

Hildr climbs off Drogon's back, her boots crunching on stone as she approaches. "That's why Naga's not here. He's gone to the dragon wasteland to fetch the other dragons."

"Don't try to attack that thing yourselves," I warn. "It is way too big for just two Valkyries and two dragons, even with magic on your side. We can't turn around and help. I don't know where it came from or what damage it has done to Elan. She needs medical help."

"I can tell." Hildr gently strokes Elan's nose, her concern-filled eyes traveling over Elan's bloodied body. "Don't worry. We have others coming to help. We were all coming to help Elan defend you, but now we will change our plan." She looks at Britta. "We'll circle the monster out of its reach and keep an eye on it. We'll make sure it doesn't come toward the populated areas while waiting for the army of waste-land dragons."

Britta nods. "From what Kara's been saying, it sounds like a good plan."

With one worry taken care of, I prepare to leave. "Great. I'd love to stay and help, but I need to get Elan back. I can feel her weakening, even though she's not admitting it."

Hildr and Britta nod in agreement. Hildr climbs back on Drogon, and I spot Drogon and Tanda staring at Elan, worry filling their eyes. Just from the way they stare at her, guilt and worry swirl through the pit of my stomach. I wish I could transport her back without her having to do all the work.

"Come on, Elan. We have to get you back to Anita and see if she can work some magic on you."

Every beat of Elan's wings fills me with worry as we head straight to the academy to seek the healer's care. Anita is an excellent healer for gods and

Valkyries but has also extended her service to dragons since they decided to join our side.

With the academy in sight, Elan lowers. Her front legs buckle under the pressure of the landing, and we almost crash face-first into the dirt outside. I jump off her back, and my boots hit the ground with a loud thud. They crunch with each hasty step toward her face. Her head collapses on the ground, and I stroke the side of her face, staring into the tiny slits of her golden-brown eyes. "Are you all right while I get Anita?"

Her nose lifts up and down once in the slightest of movements followed by a blink. It's as though speaking to me telepathically is too much effort, confirming my worst fear. I bolt inside the academy, ignoring the wide eyes of the students, and I run through the halls.

"Out of my way! Coming through!" I call as I dodge the large white wings of the winged Valkyries, finding it easier to bypass the wingless Valkyries.

As I crash through the soft white feathers of the winged Valkyries who didn't move quickly enough, I almost collide into Mistress Sigrun. Flashbacks of how mean this woman was to me swamp my thoughts as I stare into the uniformed mistress's hard face. My days in this academy were made very difficult by this woman.

Her voice booms, "Who's running through the academy halls?" Her steel-blue eyes catch sight of my face, and her expression changes. "Oh, Kara. What are you doing here?"

My tension loosens when I remember that things have changed between us since then. "I'm coming to get Anita. Elan has been attacked by a strange monster seemingly filled with lava. The beast was between the mountains not far from here. Drogon and Tanda with Hildr and Britta are keeping watch. Elan needs urgent medical attention, so I have to go. Can you send your Valkyries? They will need all the help they can get. Naga is calling the dragons from the wasteland. I don't know how long it will take them to get here."

Mistress Sigrun's face suddenly turns to business mode again. Her voice projects. "Right, Valkyries. Let's go find this monster. Gear up! Asgard needs us."

A young Valkyrie protests, "But, mistress. I haven't had enough training."

"You are Valkyrie not a human. It doesn't matter how much training you've had. The more of us out there, the more intimidating we are. Suit up!"

Her voice chases me as I run down the hall to the entrance of the healer's room.

Anita's back faces me. Her curly auburn hair is

tied into a ponytail, and she leans over a bench on the far side of the room. A wounded Valkyrie lies on her white wings on top of a gurney table. The Valkyrie's perfect face distorts in pain. Her broken limbs are evident at first glance. She thrashes in discomfort, messing her blond hair against the pillow. From my time in the academy, I know that her injuries were probably acquired by training practice.

With a furrowed brow, the wingless healer turns to her patient, her spatula still stirring the setting paste she's prepared to plaster the wound with after she's set it. After that, the Valkyrie's natural healing powers will take over and heal the break quickly. Just by Anita's casual actions, I can tell it's a menial job for an experienced healer, and although painful for the injured Valkyrie, it's not life-threatening.

"Anita!" I call.

The healer looks up, her face filled with surprise. "Kara." Quickly, her green eyes scan me as though searching for an injury. "What are you doing here?"

I'm breathless, but I push the words out as clearly as I can between pants. "It's Elan. She's been attacked by some hideous beast. It ran claws right up her scales. She needs help."

After dropping the setting paste on the bench, Anita packs a bag and charges down the corridor.

Chapter Sixteen

Anita's feet pound down the hallway behind me, dodging through the bustling Valkyries preparing for battle. Following her closely, I charge to the front door of the academy and my dragon's side.

Elan lies sprawled out, her head drooped, her unfurled wings flopping to the ground. Blood pours from underneath her scales, and my heart sinks to my feet. Worry sludges my stomach. I hope she's not mortally wounded. I don't know what I'll do without her. We have become so close over the last few years. Elan's eyes remain closed, and she's unresponsive. I muster every ounce of my energy and project it into her nose, the softest and most receptive part of her body, hoping it will help her heal.

She remains still, showing no sign of coherency. I kneel and sit on my heels, bending over her snout. My long dark hair falls on either side of my face, shielding my distress from the outside world. Her skin is cold to the touch as I clasp her nose between my hands. I shudder. Never is a dragon cold. Their fire always warms their blood.

Horrible thoughts run through my head. Panic surges inside of me. *She hasn't died, has she? Has my nightmare been realized and is manifesting? No! This can't be.* Fear wraps its talons around my heart and sinks into the flesh. It's a fear stronger than any I have felt in a battle to the death. The pain in my chest is so intense, I wonder if my own heart has stopped, refusing to push the blood through my veins. I squeeze my eyes shut. She can't give up. It would kill me. She can't be dead. Determined to manifest my wish, I hold my hands in front of her nostrils, hoping for something, some sign that she is alive and breathing, even if she's just slightly there.

"It's not good." Anita's voice leaks from the background, threatening to rip my last strand of hope away. I want to put my fingers in my ears and block it out. "These scratches have some kind of magic in them. The magic could be pulsing through her body, making it harder for her to heal."

I squeeze my eyes tighter, a movement I regrettably can't do with my ears. I attempt to ignore Anita as I concentrate only on Elan for any sign of hot air, even just a tendril of breath, to come out of her nostrils to prove that she is alive. I wait and wait. It seems to be an eternity with nothing happening. Finally, a big gush bursts out of her nostrils, pushing deep from her belly. I'm smothered in hot breath. Sweat forms on my skin. I relish it until panic clamps onto my heart, digging in its talons farther. Perhaps it's her last breath of life. I've heard that when a person dies, the last thing they do is release one large gush of air, emptying their lungs.

I hold my breath as I wait all over again for a sign of life from my beloved dragon. Another gap of time is chewed up as nothing happens. Tears well in my eyes, threatening to fall down my face. The golden scales on Elan's snout dig into my forehead, but I ignore the discomfort, waiting, hoping for her to show she's alive.

Exhausted from the emotional stress but unable to leave her side, I curl up, circling the front of her nose. I grip her snout and place my forehead in front of her nostrils. I don't want to miss any sign of life.

I whisper to her, my words catching in my emotion-clogged throat. "Elan, breathe, please." A tear trickles out of the corner of my eye and into the dirt. "Please breathe, Elan. Please. I will be nothing without you." My voice is choked with emotion, no longer sounding like me. "You will leave a gaping hole in my heart if you don't come through." My body shudders at the thought, and I curl up tighter, bringing my knees almost to the side of her nose, both of my hands still touching the tender skin. "Please, Elan. Ple—"

A massive gush pushes against my face then is sucked back into Elan's enormous form. The breath is slow and is drawn out and stops, causing my heart to skip a couple more beats. Eventually, another gush exits her nose, the flood of warm air bordering on hot, coming from deep inside Elan's belly.

My tears of sadness turn to happiness as I rejoice over the progress. "That's a girl, Elan! You keep doing that. Keep breathing," I encourage, passing on anything that may help motivate her fight through this.

The clattering of boots on the hard ground and the flapping of wings pulls my attention away. The Valkyries exit the academy and take to the sky, their white wings lining the blue, reminding me of fluffy clouds. The wingless Valkyries break into a jog toward the palace or perhaps the dragon enclosure. I wish them luck, hoping none of them will be severely injured, and turn my focus back to Elan. I should be helping protect Asgard, but I can't with my heart here with my special dragon friend.

It takes me some time before I can sit up. I've been so crippled and distraught, my brain and body struggle to move. I gather any magic left in my body and shoot the healing energy into her body, pushing it through any soft skin I can touch under her scales. My body drains wholly, and I find it hard to rise to my feet.

Eventually, I manage to stand and follow Anita around Elan. "Come on, Elan! You can do it! Fight this! Give it everything you can. You must survive this." I push more energy into her from my already-drained magic source, hoping to help, until eventually I crumple to the ground in front of her snout, resting on my back, exhausted and unable to drum up any more. I hold my hand on the soft part of her nostril. Hopefully, if she can smell me and feel me, it will bring her encouragement—a drive to go on and comfort to know that someone who cares for her is near.

The soft crunch of Anita's footsteps breaks into my consciousness as she circles Elan, plastering healing salve on her wounds, working some of her healing magic into her.

I remain next to Elan, slowly gathering my energy, my thoughts lost in scenarios on how to help her. I try to break through the clouds of exhaustion crowding my brain. I need to find someone on Asgard who has the power of healing magic. Gilroma said that he had taught Anita healing magic, but did he teach her everything? I'll have to wait and see. I remain next to Elan's nose, the steady soft breath the only thread of hope I feel.

Anita works quietly in the background, her brow knitted together and worry filling her eyes. Eventually, she collapses next to me with her legs crossed. She tucks a strand of dark hair behind her ear. "Are you all right, Kara?"

It takes all of my effort to nod.

Concern fills her eyes, and her gaze looks unconvinced as the creases on her forehead deepen. Her flawless face scrunches up as she pouts her lips. "I've covered every wound with a special potion. It's a potion that Gilroma taught me. I'm hoping this will heal her along with the little healing magic I know. My knowledge isn't extensive." She stares into the distance. "If it doesn't work, then we'll have to find someone else to help her."

My throat is dry, and I struggle to talk. I croak out the words. "Is Gilroma's healing magic stronger?" I attempt to push myself up from the ground and prop my body up with my elbows. Failing, I flop back down, my arms sprawling out to the sides. "Is he able to heal wounds as bad as this?"

Serious eyes gaze down at me. "That depends on what kind of magic this creature used. Do you know what this creature is?"

I shake my hand. "No. It's something I've never

seen or heard of before. I'm planning on visiting the library to see if we have any records of it at the academy." I try to swallow to moisten my dry throat but receive little relief. "This creature is enormous. Extremely big, and it is black all over with feet bigger than Elan's head. When it opens its mouth and eyes, they are full of a lava type of flame, burning red and bright. When Elan gouged its torso, the same kind of flames showed through its wounds. It looks pure evil and nasty. Have you heard of something like that before?" Slowly, I prop myself up then collapse again.

She shakes her head. Her eyes fill with sadness again. "Then, I don't know if my magic will help."

Tears threaten to burst from my eyes. "If your magic isn't enough, then who can we call?"

"We can always visit Loki." Her face looks distant and sad as she says this, her gaze falling to the ground. "After all, he and Gilroma are one and the same."

A sudden burst of energy shoots to my core, and I attempt to sit up again, pushing off my elbows. This time I succeed in getting halfway up and prop myself there. "I wouldn't trust a word that came out of that god's mouth."

"I know." She shrugs. "But he may be someone

who has answers. He holds powerful magic when he's in the form of Gilroma, and he trained me."

Despite my disgust for how he treated and deceived me, along with the rest of Asgard, he marked me with his magic. Absentmindedly, I stroke the scar on my shoulder, where the zmey struck me. It spikes the memory of the pain that coursed through the scar before my magic manifested. Not only that, he also marked my friends with the same magic. He was training all of us before he betrayed our realm. Which makes it harder to comprehend where his loyalties lie. Knowing all of this, it still makes it impossible for me to like Loki. The last act of deception created so much distrust, I can't move past it.

"Is there anyone else we can ask?" I search the healer's face for some glimmer of hope.

Anita hesitates. "There is someone else or another race that we can ask."

"Who?"

"The light elves. They know the magic of the dark elves. They know just as much magic as Gilroma did."

"But I thought the light elves are peaceful creatures that do little more than be happy and focus on the light."

Anita huffs in amusement. "The dark elves that

invaded Asgard are light elves that turned bad. The true dark elves are more like the ones that represent what some humans call dwarves. They live deep inside the mountain, and the light elves live on top, close to the light and sun. The light elves that turned, which you know as dark elves, live somewhere else entirely. Even the purest of souls can be turned if they have darkness in their hearts."

I groan. "I'm so confused. I thought what invaded Asgard were dark elves." I stare at Anita, flicking the dirt underneath my hand with my fingernail.

"That was a misconception. In any case, the point we are trying to cover is that the light elves should know the same magic as Gilroma." Anita looks into the distance again. "Except, to reach the light elves would be an extensive trip, and Loki is local. I'm not sure how long Elan will last. You need to get her healed quickly."

"I really don't want to see Loki at the moment, maybe even ever again." I expel a large sigh. "I'm not happy, but I guess he's my best choice at the moment."

Chapter Seventeen

I wait, hoping Elan will get better soon. If she doesn't show any improvement in the next few minutes, I'll have to leave. Her large eyes remain sealed shut, and her head still slumps on the ground. I hug her snout and rest my cheek on her scales. "Come on, Elan. Get better and wake up. You can do it. Fight this magic, and push it out of your body."

A soft, comforting hand rests on my shoulder. I peer up to find Anita bending over me. I was so focused on Elan, I didn't know she stood up.

She rubs my upper back gently in a circle. "I'm going to do another round and check on her wounds."

I nod, not bothering to push past the lump in my throat to answer her.

Anita walks around Elan's enormous form, investigating every wound and every magical poultice she's applied to them. There are so many wounds on her vast body that it takes quite some time. Several minutes pass before she finally returns to where I sit.

Clinging onto my final hope, I gaze into her green eyes, searching for confirmation of improvement, but they are clouded with sorrow and regret, crushing any optimism I hold.

"They're not getting any better. You're going to have to find someone with stronger magic."

I cringe, my stomach churning. Elan's going through all of this because she was trying to protect me. If only she had turned invisible and hid from the lava monster instead of standing against it alone.

A loud roar, answered by dragon roars, echoes through the valley toward the academy. Shrill cries of Valkyries pierce the air, followed by another roar. That has to be more than a couple of dragons. The dragons from the wastelands must've arrived. This lifts my spirits slightly, but they're crushed again when I gaze back at Elan's unmoving form.

A moment later, the rumble of a carriage draws my attention, and I see Thor passing, his carriage pulled by his goats, Tanngrisnir and Tanngnjostr. The sunshine illuminates the red in Thor's unruly hair and beard as he charges past the academy, heading straight toward the fight scene. The goats' speed is impressive for such tiny creatures. Behind the carriage, an extensive line of gods follow him, their muscled bodies intimidating as they jog in a group toward the battle. Each god that passes raises my hopes of destroying this monster.

Minutes later, lightning flashes from the sky, darting down to Thor's hammer then back into the sky. Thor is warming up Mjollnir, ready for battle. Surely they must have a chance against this lava monster.

By herself, Elan had no chance. I don't know why she took on this monster alone. It's not like her to take foolish chances. Maybe she didn't have a choice because it appeared out of nowhere.

When I look back at Elan, her lack of movement breaks my heart all over again. I turn a questioning gaze toward Anita. She shakes her head, sorrow filling her eyes. My insides turn to mush as the defeat of Elan's recovery takes over my body. The only hope left is to travel to the light elves, a trip that could take too long, or do the unthinkable. Either way, I can't leave Elan the way she is.

With a heavy heart, I brace my out-of-control emotions and ask Anita the inconceivable. "Do you know where I can find Loki?"

A pang of guilt gnaws at me. I haven't visited the unruly god since he was chained under the serpent's venom. On the other hand, I'm proud that I haven't visited the god who acted like my friend then deceived me and, to some degree, left me feeling as though I was the reason Asgard was put in danger. It hurt me to think that he was my friend in many forms, yet each friendship was a big fat lie.

A strand of curly red hair falls out of her ponytail, and Anita slowly hooks it behind her ear then nods. A strange kind of sympathy flashes through her eyes, as though she read my thoughts, as though she could see deep down into the pit of my soul. "He has done much to me, too, Kara. I know where you're coming from, and I know how hard this is. But it may be Elan's only chance."

I cringe from the fate of those words—to be so desperate that I must rely on my enemy.

"He is trapped in the dungeons deep underneath the castle."

I frown. "The dungeons aren't that deep. I've been there to rescue Elan."

"The normal palace dungeons aren't deep, but they are not the ones I am talking about. These dungeons reside deep within the confines of the realm, buried well within the rocks." Anita's shoulders cave. "It's not a pleasant place. If you thought the palace dungeons were bad, this is almost like living with the undead. I have been once to supply him with salve to help heal his flesh from the burns of the venom. That's all. I don't think he deserves any more than that." She runs a hand gently over Elan's golden scales, love and care radiating from her face. "I can't come with you."

I nod my understanding.

"It's going to be dangerous going down to visit Loki. I was accompanied by guards because my visit was approved by Odin. There are many creatures down there that may attack you. Do you know anyone who could go with you?"

The lava monster roars, and chills run down my spine. The shrillness of the Valkyrie cry follows along with the roar of the combined dragons. Lightning illuminates the sky, and dark, intimidating clouds cluster over the battle.

"Probably everybody I know is in the battle right now, and I don't want to take anyone away from defeating that monster. Asgard's safety is also important."

"I can't come with you," Anita says again, this time almost a hushed whisper. "I wish I could. But I have to stay here because I'm the main healer. There may be many who will need healing from the battle."

I nod. "I understand. I wouldn't expect any more from you." I take another long look at Elan, contemplating what I'm about to do. I ready my weary body, exhausted from pumping every bit of energy into her. It has slowly been recharging but not fast enough. I can only hope it is restored before I reach the dangerous area on my journey. Even if it doesn't, I'm doing this for Elan whether I'm ready or not.

Behind me, something thuds on the ground. I spin to face Naga with Eir mounted on his back. Both their faces look distraught as they observe Elan's state.

"Oh, Vanir!" Eir says. "What happened?"

"The lava monster got her. The creature imbued some kind of magic in her wounds. She's not healing."

"Oh, Kara." Eir climbs off Naga's back. "Is there anything I can do?"

I shake my head. "I've pumped every bit of power into her that I can. I'm drained, and I don't think it's done any good. Anita has applied a magic salve, and the wounds are still not healing. It looks as though I need the magic of the dark elves. I need Gilroma's magic to help Elan."

Eir's hand freezes over Elan's scales, her face stunned. "How can you do that?"

"I'm going to have to visit Loki. Whatever happens from there will happen."

Eir's mouth drops open. "You're not going to set him free, are you?"

"No! There's no way I'm going to set him free." My voice is high-pitched. I sigh, and my shoulders droop. "To be honest, I don't know what's going to happen. Whatever happens, happens, but I must keep a close eye on him because I don't want him to go unpunished. I just know I have to get his magic to Elan. If he can't transport healing magic through me, then I must get it to her somehow."

Naga and Eir will come with you. Naga's big blue compassionate eyes melt my heart. I stroke Naga's snout, and he leans into me, closing his eyes briefly before glancing up at me with that heartwarming expression.

"I would love that, Naga, but I don't know how I'm going to sneak a dragon past the guards at the castle. They will let me in and possibly Eir also, but I don't think they will let a dragon in, even a smaller one. I think they will become suspicious if we try to get you in as well. They may stop us from entering."

Naga's big blue eyes flicker with understanding. He nods once. *Then Naga will stay with Elan. Naga will watch over her.*

"Thank you, Naga." I expel a sigh, happy to know that Elan will have a dragon for company. I gaze at Eir. "Are you sure you want to come?"

Eir's peaceful face breaks into a smile. "Of course. I'm helping a friend. That's a good reason to cause a little mischief."

Chapter Eighteen

L eaving Naga by Elan's side, Eir and I make our way to the palace, the opposite direction of the battle with the monster. Without our dragons, the progress is slow, and we break into a run. Each step I take is difficult without my full strength, but my concern for Elan pushes me on, our warrior-trained bodies devouring the distance quickly.

When we arrive, I press my back against a building, my chest heaving, and I peer around the corner, assessing which guards stand at attention at the palace entrance. I wipe my brow, relieved to see Gorm and Birger aren't on break. Still, I know it might take a bit to talk my way in when everyone else is at the battle.

My energy hasn't returned to its full potential, but I don't have the luxury of waiting. I speak over my shoulder. "I'm going to have to talk our way in. Let's go."

Our footsteps echo against the walls as we approach the front door, portraying the air of urgency.

We march up the steps, and Gorm holds out his hand. "Halt!"

My teeth clamp together, and my heart thumps rapidly against my rib cage. Hopefully, I can pull this off.

"What are you two doing here? The battle is on the other side." The guard points in the direction of the different dragon sounds and the monster roaring. A bolt of lightning flashes down from the sky as though pinpointing the location.

I put my weight on one leg and toss my hand, expressing disbelief. "Thor forgot something and sent me back for it."

Birger huffs. "Typical. What did he forget?"

"He forgot his belt. Would you believe it?" I roll my eyes to emphasize the point. "He will need every bit of energy to defeat this monster."

Birger's eyebrows rise, and tension grips my throat as I worry that they won't believe me. "That's a strange thing to forget, but he definitely needs that."

Gorm indicates Eir. "And what's she doing here?"

I can feel the blood drain from my face, and I turn

away from them, hoping they won't notice as I try to conjure the reason Eir is with me.

Eir's sweet, smooth voice brings me hope as she explains, "Kara lost a lot of energy throwing magic at that monster. I'm here to help her carry the belt. Have you ever felt how heavy it is?"

Gorm shakes his head. "No. Although, I've heard it's rather heavy. I don't know how Thor carries all that heavy weaponry all the time."

Birger calls to Gorm, "Let them go. They must be in a hurry. Thor needs that belt." He stands aside, and Gorm follows suit, letting us pass.

I smile, trying to hide my relief. "Thank you. I'd hate to go back empty-handed."

We hurry inside and down the corridors, passing through the passageways and quickly out of Gorm's and Birger's sight. We check swiftly for any guards when we reach the entrance to the lower levels. It would be impossible to explain to any guards that I took a wrong turn to Thor's room when they know I've visited Thor a lot over the last couple of years.

We follow the white marbled hallways farther down, trying to contain the noise of our hurried footprints and staggered breaths that bounce off the stone walls. It's an effort not to run when Elan's life is hanging in the balance and we need to get Loki's help as soon as possible.

I'm reminded just how important it is to observe every direction when two guards march down the next corridor, heading our way. I grind to a halt. Eir slams into the back of me, almost pushing me into the open. Quickly, I back up, and we press our backs against the wall, hoping they avoid our corridor and march straight to another part of the castle.

The footsteps approach, closer and closer, causing my heart to beat harder. I ball my fist, trying to steady my nerves, my mind running through a million different excuses. I need a logical explanation to tell them if they find us. My breath hitches as the marching footsteps approach then continue down the corridor, missing our turn altogether. My legs turn to jelly momentarily. I know how close we came to being caught.

From then on, I pause at every corner before entering another room or level, making sure no one is watching us. Eventually, we pass the kitchen and scullery and move deeper beneath the palace into the dungeons. This area is familiar to me, as I snuck down here when Elan was held prisoner by Odin. It was a horrible place then, and it's an awful place now.

Different creatures and people peer at us through the bars of their locked cells. I can't help checking every dungeon to make sure there are no dragons or anybody who shouldn't be there. Although Odin seems to have changed over the last couple of years, I still wonder at times if it's just a face. Now is the perfect time to check. To my satisfaction, every prisoner seems to be legitimate. At the same time, I check to make sure that Loki hasn't been brought up to this level. Anita hasn't visited him since the early days of him being imprisoned.

Different creatures snap at us through the bars as we walk past, and dark elves stare at us eerily, their hands bound by some kind of magic-dampening cuffs. They must be some of the warriors that attacked Asgard a couple of years ago.

After covering most of the dungeon, I haven't spotted any way out other than the entrance. A monster's snout sticks through the bars and snaps its jaws at us. Eir and I dart to the other side, careful not to back into another snapping creature in the cell behind us. Our footsteps grow less confident as we come up empty-handed, yet determination pushes us on. Anita wouldn't have lied to us. We reach the farthest corner that lurks in the dark, and I'm surprised yet happy to find a door hidden in the darkness.

A silent exchange passes between Eir and me. We know this has to be the entrance to the lower levels. I clasp the handle, yank it down, and pull the door open. Stairs descend immediately from the door, leading down into darkness, occasionally lit by the dull light of a sconce. A creepy feeling travels up my spine to the base of my skull. We haven't even entered the area. This isn't going to be fun.

Eir's face drains of color when I motion for her to follow. Her eyes fix on the darkness below.

"I know," I whisper. "I'm not looking forward to this either."

Despite manifesting her fear and the desire to withdraw, she tiptoes behind me, and we descend the stairs. Each time my boot hits a hard step, the noise seems to explode through the small enclosed area, spilling into the space below. I cringe, trying to make each step softer. We have no idea if there are guards or monsters below.

We go farther down the stairs that seem to never end until finally, they stop. I halt, peeking around the corner before we enter. The layout of the room appears to be designed to give the occupants the upper hand. They have an opportunity to ambush the new arrivals before the new arrivals know of their presence.

After surveying the room, I face Eir. The whites of her wide eyes glow in the sconce's mild light. Even though I couldn't find anyone in the room, I feel the same as how Eir looks about going into the room. Despite her fear, she nods, indicating she is ready to go. I grapple for my sword, taking some comfort in knowing it's by my side, and I face the direction we need to go. I'm about to step into the room when suddenly Eir grabs my shoulder and yanks me back. My sword scrapes against the rock.

Puzzled, I turn to look at Eir. I hadn't spotted anything moving. As our eyes connect, she shakes her head and points to my sword before circling her hand in front of her.

She whispers, "Magic."

I lift my eyebrows at her.

"We don't want to injure anybody," she whispers again.

I contemplate the idea for a moment. My body still isn't fully recovered from giving Elan everything I have. I feel for my power and how much I think I have available to use then nod and slide my sword back into the sheath on my back. Together we pause and gather our magic. When Eir indicates to me that she is ready, we move forward, our hands lifted in front of our torsos, prepared to block or attack.

The room borders on dark, the limited dull light making it hard to see. My senses are on full alert until my eyes adjust better to the obscurity. Every corner of the room screams eeriness. Only the center is illuminated with a dull light. I can't see anything a foot in front of my face, but I press forward, an image of Elan's unmoving body spurring me on.

My eyes take too long to adjust, and I feel sick with insecurity as I press farther into the darkness, afraid for my life and Eir's. If guards were down here, I would think that they would have accosted us by now, but none have approached.

Holding my breath, we shuffle farther forward, unsure if we should move into the light or stick to the darkness just in case the light aids some creature in attacking us. Then again, it might be a creature that can see in the dark. That thought does not bring me peace. Hopefully, if something is waiting to attack, we have been quiet enough to sneak in.

I opt to stay out of the circle of light, knowing the passageway we need to find to the next room is not lit. It takes too long for my eyes to adjust to the darkness, and I curse under my breath. A strange, dense, musty odor mixed with something else assaults my nose. I'm not quite sure what it is, although it reminds me of the corpse smell that clings to the angels of death. It's something I haven't smelled in a very long time, not since I went to Midgard with the winged Valkyries. Thor has had other plans for me lately instead of reaping souls. The smell intensifies with each shuffle forward through the dark. Suddenly, my foot knocks something on the ground. I freeze.

Chapter Nineteen

Clasping Eir behind me, I squeeze her hand with so much pressure that I can feel her apprehension manifest.

Her hands grasp my arms, and she pulls close, whispering in my ear, "What is it?"

I hiss my response. "There's something on the ground."

"Maybe it's what's causing that horrid stench." Her breath tickles my ear, sparking my sensations and causing me to shudder.

"Whatever it is, I don't believe this is where Loki is."

"I don't think so either. I don't know that there's anything alive in this room. And that smell..." She sniffs then chokes, expelling a muffled cough. "May be something dead."

"I need to see what's at my feet. There may be more on the floor, and somehow, we need to find the door in this darkness. There must be one in here leading to Loki's area. Not to mention, I would love to see what we are dealing with."

I think I hear her chuckle. "Then, I guess now is a good time to show you the new trick I've learned."

"What do you mean?"

She lets go of my arm, and if it weren't for the incredibly dull light in the middle of the room, I would have felt disorientated. The light doesn't even illuminate our skin.

"Watch," she whispers.

I wait in the darkness, apprehension gnawing at my stomach. Suddenly, a ball of flame from the dimly burning sconce in the middle of the room shoots toward us. Thinking I'm a target, I dodge to the side, trying not to move my feet because of the thing on the floor. The light veers to my right at the last second and straight onto Eir's outstretched palm. It hovers over her cupped hand as though drawn to it.

My wide-eyed gaze slides between her illuminated face and the flame. "When did you learn to do that?" I whisper, not sure why as I'm certain that if anything were in this room, it would know we are here by now, especially after the display of light.

Her eyes flick up from her creation, pride filling her expression. "While you all have been practicing war moves with your magic, I've been practicing things that might be helpful for a peaceful environment, like accessing light and moving the light source when needed." She shrugs. "I had fun with this one."

I'm so happy, I want to hug her, but the pressing issue of what's on the floor still haunts me. Eir holds the light close to the ground and creeps around me. Her light reveals a person's foot then crawls up its leg to a fully clothed body. My stomach heaves as I take in the decaying form, the skin on its face clinging to its bone. Whoever it was, they've been dead for a while, and they're wearing a guard uniform.

Eir gags. "This isn't good. Whatever killed them could still be in this room or below."

"Yup. I realize that, but if we are going to help Elan, I have to press on." I swallow my fear and disgust one final time and follow Eir as she searches for the opening of another door with her illuminated palm.

We slowly make our way around the walls of the large room, our senses on full alert for any other corpses or any other disgusting or dangerous things.

Finally, I spot another door on the far back wall. With her palm held high, Eir opens the door, the hinges squeaking from lack of use, and we gape into the darkness.

Eir whispers over her shoulder, "This must be the way."

I nod, not wanting to speak, and we press forward. I clasp the back of her belt wrapped around her black leathers, making sure I don't lose her. I hate the thought of my peaceful friend going first. I feel as though I'm putting her in more danger than myself, but I have no choice. I don't know how to do the little trick with the light like she does. So without protest, I keep close as we press forward, keeping my eyes peeled for anything that moves.

Our progress is slow as we creep farther into the depths of the darkness. Our leather fighting clothes creak and scratch as they catch on rocks in the tiny tunnels. Eir's sheathed sword clangs against the rocks, and we both jump, pressing on as soon as we realize the cause of the noise. I gather my magic, ready to combat anything that may be lurking in the darkness that's ready to attack us. The trek through the darkness seems endless as we go through another level and another room. Finally, we come across a small pocket of light that glows dully up ahead.

I tap Eir on the shoulder and point in its direction. She nods, and we aim slowly for the light, checking the floor to make sure nothing will sink away and drop off into a chasm or some other kind of nasty surprise between us and the light. I don't like this one bit, but with the image of an unconscious Elan in my head, I press on. I must make sure my dragon survives and things get back to the way they should be. Not only should I be out there fighting this monster, but I should also be by Elan's side.

My nerves are firing as we approach. Strange noises echo back to us, not helping my heart to settle. We reach the entrance, and slowly, ensuring our footsteps are silent, we creep around the corner into the room.

My jaw slackens. Not far in the distance, Loki is strung in place under a sizeable hanging serpent. Poison drips from its fangs. His wife, Sigyn, holds a bowl under the serpent's head, attempting to catch each drop of poison before it drops onto Loki's bare skin.

I had heard whispers that when she pulls the bowl away to empty the contents, the consistently dripping venom would land on Loki. The god would writhe in pain, causing the earth to shake with a violent earthquake as his howl of pain and distress rumbled throughout the land.

I search the room, only finding Loki and his wife, and I press forward, with Eir following. Slowly, I move to stand in front of Loki. The dark-haired god is in his Asgard form and stripped to his underwear, undoubtedly a ploy to leave much of his skin exposed to the venom, inflicting as much pain as possible. The punishment looks cruel, way beyond how anyone should be treated, whatever they have done. Disgust churns in my stomach to know that this is what the gods of Asgard have done to him. I can understand the hatred, but this I cannot. Even though I no longer trust him, it seems rather extreme.

Sigyn follows our progress with a strange look in her eye, her face deadpan and unemotional. Loki must catch the stiffness in her body and glances up at her before following her line of sight.

I halt in shock as I take in his sunken eyes, difficult to see between the dark rings that circle them. It looks as though he hasn't slept for the last two years. His face is drawn, and his body is frail. He doesn't look like the god that he used to be up above, full of life and mischief. I worry about his strength and his ability to heal Elan in his frail state. I hope he has enough energy to transfer his healing power to me.

"Kara. Eir. How nice of you to come and visit," Loki drawls, low with an undercurrent of spite, a tone that I understand after seeing the way he's been treated.

Hesitantly I press on. "This isn't how I imagined the gods would punish you, Loki. I never thought they would be this cruel. Despite what you've done to them, Asgard, my friends, and…" I inhale deeply, trying to release some of the pain before I say the truth. "Me. You were like my best friend in many different forms. For quite some time, I confided in you things I never expressed to my true friends, and you deceived me."

Another drop of venom drips from the serpent fangs, and I watch as Sigyn just manages to catch it in time.

I continue, "Yet, I never would have thought of this punishment in a million years."

One side of Loki's mouth lifts in a sarcastic smile. "They thrive on punishing in terrifying ways. The gods of Asgard have vivid imaginations when it comes to torturing people or things."

I press my tongue to the roof of my mouth. I don't like the way they treated him, but at the same time, I still have a deep rage burning through me over his deception.

Noting our silence, Loki continues, "I was working for Asgard, you know. I realize a lot of you don't believe me. In fact, all of you don't believe me." He huffs. "And to think I went through so much for Asgard." He shakes his head.

I growl. "You brought the dark elves to our land. You split the dragons, stealing their eggs and turning their babies against their mothers and family. How was that for Asgard?"

Something flashes through his eyes. "You wouldn't believe me if I told you."

I shake my head, attempting to clear away his taunting and his baiting, trying to remember precisely why I'm here. An image of Elan enters my thoughts, and instantly I remember. I blurt it out before this unpleasant conversation progresses. "I need you to help me."

His dark eyebrow arches. "And what's in it for me?"

Chapter Twenty

"What's in it for you?" I almost yell at him. "You deceived me in every way you could. You don't deserve anything for that. You should want to help me and make amends for everything you've done." I place all my weight on one leg and cross my arms over my chest.

Sigyn stares at us, her face distressed as she contemplates what I've said. Suddenly Loki cries out in pain, and he starts to shake. His limbs pull on his restraints. The rock walls shudder and vibrate. Small rocks clatter from the ceiling to the rock floor.

With wide eyes, I survey the room, hoping that the walls will hold and it won't cave in on us.

Horror washes over Sigyn's face as she realizes that she has moved the bowl and missed the last drop of venom. She quickly moves the container underneath the serpent's head, stopping the poisonous liquid from dripping on Loki's skin again.

It takes a while for Loki to gain control over his body, allowing the walls of the cave to stop their shaking, leaving a wake of scattered rocks on the floor. He glares at his wife, and she cringes.

"I'm sorry." Her voice is small, weak from the exertion of constantly holding the bowl to protect him and knowing she failed for the briefest of moments, causing her husband pain.

Loki closes his eyes slowly, each breath gradual and controlled as the anger eventually washes away. He nods. "It must be hard holding the bowl still all the time. Your arms must be aching."

A sadness envelops her face. "It is hard. But not as much as you bearing the snake's venom on your skin." Her concerned eyes skim to us. "Perhaps you should help them, Loki."

Loki gazes at us, then his gaze travels up to the snake hovering over the bowl. As though watching his every move with a malicious interest, the serpent moves its head directly in line with Loki's face. Sigyn quickly shoves the bowl between them as another drop of venom leaves the serpent's mouth, and Loki returns his gaze to us.

"Fine. I'll help you. What do you need help with?"

"Elan has been injured by some kind of lava monster." A lump rises in my throat, and my voice cracks as I struggle to get the words past it. "She could die if we don't heal her." I swallow, trying to clear the emotional blockage that threatens to make me cry. I must be strong for Elan. "Anita can't combat the unfamiliar magic that travels through Elan's veins, inhibiting her from healing."

Loki nods in understanding. "I should be able to help you, but there's one problem. I can't do anything from here. I have to be touching the dragon, and I know you can't bring her down here." He tilts his head toward the small entrance of the cave. "She's too big, and if she's as bad as you say, she won't make it."

I gape at him. "I can't break you out! Can't you pass some magic on to me that I can carry to the surface or teach me some magic to perform on her?"

He shakes his head. "I'm sorry. I can't. It's too complicated to teach, and it's not transferrable. To be honest, I could use a day trip."

I scowl. "Odin won't allow it!"

A smirk spreads across his face. "I know you say you don't want to go against Odin's rules, but I don't believe Odin would let anybody down here to visit me." He gives me a sly look. "I'm guessing you've bypassed him."

Unintentionally, I gaze down at the ground. That's all the acknowledgment he needs.

"I assumed as much." He tries to sit up but fails, slumping back to the ground with annoyance. "I like your dragon. She has spunk, and she must be in a bad way if you came all the way down here, breaking rules, to see me." His pale and clammy face loses all pretense. "But I simply can't do it from here."

Loki's voice is genuine, and it stirs all kinds of emotions through my gut. I don't know where else to go for Elan in such a short period, and I can't take him to the surface without Odin's permission. Looking for answers, I glance at Eir.

"I don't like the sound of this," Eir whispers. Her face is drawn, and her concerned eyes flash to Loki. "But I don't know what else to do."

I follow her gaze, contemplating my next move. I don't like the sound of it either. It's twisting my stomach into knots, disrupting every bit of peace within me. If I take him with me and I'm caught, I'll be in so much trouble, I don't know if I'll be able to redeem myself.

The image of Elan lying still, her eyes closed, shoots into my vision, and I squirm. That dragon is dear to my heart. I can't let her die like this.

I fix my earnest eyes on him. "Elan was struck by something. We don't know where it came from or what it is. This creature is black, taller than her. When its eyes or mouth open, it looks as though it's filled with lava. Do you honestly think you can heal her from this creature's wounds?"

"I cannot guarantee such a thing, but I do believe that Gilroma's magic will give your dragon the best chance in the shortest amount of time. One thing I can guarantee is that her recovery time is crucial. To seek out anyone else to help heal her will take too long."

I gnaw my bottom lip, weighing my options. Eir shrugs when I cast her a worried look.

I hold up a threatening finger toward him. "No funny business!"

"I would never." An innocent smile spreads across his face, and I cringe.

I don't have much choice. I know it would be best to ask Odin for permission to transport Loki to see Elan and for his help in securing the mischievous god while he is out. Except, Odin hasn't been the same since he received that vision. He would never grant permission for Loki to roam, even to help one dragon who he holds in high regard. With sweaty palms, I reach for my magically blessed sword and begin cutting at the ties that bind Loki.

"You'll have to be quick," Loki says. "These ties alert the guards that I've escaped. They'll be here within moments."

I cringe, slicing my sword across the binds faster.

The damage is already done. "You could've told me that before I started." His hand slides free, and I work on the second binding.

"I have an idea to help buy us some time."

I release Loki's second hand from its ties, and he rubs his wrists.

"Do you have some parchment and a pen?" he asks.

"I do." Eir fishes in her leathers to pull them out.

After squatting by Loki's legs, I give Eir a strange look. It's an odd thing for a Valkyrie to carry.

Eir holds the items out for Loki and catches my expression. She smirks and shrugs. "You like to read. I like to write."

"Thank you." Loki clasps Eir's items and scribbles on the parchment while I work on releasing his feet. His legs slide free, and he jumps up, ducking away from the serpent's head and placing the parchment on the spot where he was sitting.

I read the contents.

I'll be back shortly. Just taking a short trip. Thanks for the pleasant accommodation. Loki.

I lift my eyebrows at him. "Interesting. But I don't think this will excuse what we're doing."

Loki shrugs and smirks.

We charge up the levels the way Eir and I arrived, working our way through the entrances as quickly as possible and assisting Loki when he looks frail. The passage through the horrible room with the dead guard is much quicker than on our way down, and I'm glad.

A rumble of voices echoes through the darkness. We find a gap large enough for us to press against the wall and watch the guards charge toward Loki's room. When the guards are gone, we press on, trying to reach the top of the palace before being discovered.

Light streams through a door, and I'm grateful for the assistance. I push it open, checking every direction before entering the dungeon.

A cloak lies on a table in the corner of the room, and Loki grabs it, sliding his arms through the sleeves. "It's so nice to finally have some kind of clothing. I'm a little tired of always being in my underwear."

I screw up my nose at the reminder and push it out of my thoughts. "Shh. I have to focus," I hiss.

Eir passes me, indicating with her hands that she'll scout ahead and check for guards. Hiding just inside the entrance of the dungeon, I watch her tiptoe across the floor, dodging the vicious animals in their cells, her boots silent on the stones. She reaches the far side and, after peering around the corner, motions for us to follow. We make it to the ground level of the palace, and I cringe as I eye the guards at the front door. I see no way to sneak past the two guards.

"There is a back way, you know," Loki says.

I stare at him in disbelief. "And you're telling me this now? What're we waiting for? Let's go."

Loki leads us in the opposite direction, and we escape out the back doors of the palace. Despite looking frail and starved, Loki manages to keep up a good pace to the academy.

My heart skips a beat when I spot Naga curled up next to Elan. With his head resting on his talons and his body turned our direction, he watches us with concerned eyes as we approach.

Hearing our footsteps, Anita spins. Relief floods her face when she spots me but is replaced with a look of ice when she sees Loki. "You helped him escape?"

"Not escape. He'll be going back. I ran through several scenarios. There was no other way to do it. He needs access to Elan to be able to heal her wounds."

The respected wingless Valkyrie healer pauses for a moment, processing the information, then nods. "Yes, that would be true."

Anita's eyes narrow as she stands back and watches Loki transform into Gilroma. The resemblance to Loki is nonexistent. All signs of hair disappear from his head, leaving a bald scalp, the forehead inked with prongs resembling a trident. Glowing yellow eyes land on me.

My skin crawls. As though sensing it, Anita wraps an arm around my shoulders, a reminder that I'm not the only one who has suffered at the hands of Gilroma.

Slowly, Gilroma circles Elan's unmoving body and investigates her injuries. I can't pull my eyes away from the tattooed lines down his cheeks and the inked points showing the way to the scars that run all the way to his thin mouth. Gilroma tugs at the double-looped earrings on the lobe of his pointed ear before he runs his hands along the damaged scales. His touch is a caress as he senses the magic that lies within her wounds underneath her scales. Gently rubbing his hands over the wounds in a circular motion, he mutters incantations as he paces ever so slowly around her body, addressing one injury at a time.

I cross my fingers and my toes, looking for reassurance from Anita, hoping and praying to the gods that this will work.

.

Chapter Twenty-One

Perspiration gathers on my forehead, and I wring my hands on my lap as I wait for Loki to finish. I tune into each movement Elan makes, assessing every breath, hoping for a flicker of an eyelid. Gilroma's healing is taking too long for my aching heart.

Elan shows no sign of healing, and I slump down to my knees and embrace her snout. Wet tears well in my eyes and drip down my face, falling onto her golden scales. "I hate seeing you this way, Elan. Please, get better. Please," I plead.

Gilroma's footsteps move behind me, circling my body as I lean against my precious golden dragon's snout. His mutterings and incantations follow him as he continues his rounds of the enormous emperor dragon, his hands continually touching her wounds.

On both my sides, rocks clatter as two warm bodies crumple next to me. Soft hands caress my shoulders and back. In my grief, I lose count of how many times Gilroma circles Elan. Many or few, I don't know. My mind is lost, focusing purely on Elan. Right now, nothing else matters.

My concentration is broken momentarily as Sigyn announces, "I'm going to get my hair done. I've been stuck down there for so long."

I don't bother to respond, and I don't know if anyone else acknowledges her before her footsteps rattle through the rocks as she backs away.

I snuggle into Elan's snout, begging for her to heal and wake up. I have violated the sacred trust of Odin and Thor by breaking Loki out, yet this means nothing in comparison to Elan's health.

Hot steam bursts from Elan's nostrils, and I push away from her. Eir and Anita do the same, and we narrowly miss scalding our skin.

Elan's eyelids flutter rapidly until, eventually, they pause half-open, and her pupils focus on me.

Hello you. Why are you looking so glum? Elan's voice sounds groggy in my head, but I can hear the dampened cheek.

I raise an eyebrow and don't bother hiding my sarcasm. "Maybe because I'm worried about a certain dragon."

And what dragon would that be? she continues, her

voice sounding croaky even in my head. *That particular dragon wouldn't be me, would it?*

I smile and knock my fist softly on her snout. "Of course it's you, silly. I would be lost without you." I wipe away the wetness on my cheeks and gaze at her through moist eyes.

Naga jumps to his feet and trots excitedly on the spot. *Naga's happy to see you, Elan. Naga's so happy to see your eyes open.* Naga nudges Elan in a place that wasn't injured.

The relief through my body is euphoric, and I can't take my eyes off her moving form.

So, did we beat the monster? Elan asks.

I straighten my spine, sitting on my heels, and turn in the direction that I know the fight would be taking place. I had completely forgotten about the monster and the battle to defeat it. Lightning doesn't pierce the sky, and air lacks the war cries of the Valkyries and the roar of the dragons. I swallow. "I hope so, but to be honest, I wouldn't know. I was so worried about you and running down to get Loki."

Loki! Elan gapes at me like I'm insane. *Why would you need him?*

"To heal you, silly." I nudge her again. "Anita's healing magic wasn't enough, so I had to get more experienced help quickly. Gilroma was the only one I could think of."

The scales buckle in the middle of her forehead as she frowns. *That was risky.* Lazily she looks around, her eyes surveying the area. *So, where is he now?*

"What?" I jump to my feet and circle her. She's right. There is no sign of Loki anywhere. "Oh, Vanir! That lying, deceiving god!"

It takes me a long time to see past my burning anger, every curse under the sun racing through my head. The blood drains from my face, and my legs start to quiver. All the happiness over Elan's safety washes away in a matter of seconds.

Eir, Anita, and Naga help me search, each of us coming up fruitless.

"Where do we search now?" The tension causes my voice to rise in pitch.

All of us turn several times, five sets of eyes scanning for any movement over the horizon.

"Oh, this is bad." I can almost hear the tremble of disappointment, anger, and fear of Odin's wrath in Anita's voice.

"I'm responsible," I say.

Anita's eyes fill with sadness. "It's kind of my fault also."

I shake my head. "No. I'm the one who released him, and I'm the one who's going to take the punishment." I growl. "And these last two years have been spectacular having Odin and Thor's trust. I have to find him soon, or I could be the one chained up underneath the mountains with venom dripping off *my* face, or worse." I chortle nervously.

In the distance, a flock of white flies our way, and my heart skips a beat when I realize it's the winged Valkyries heading back to the academy.

Eir claps her hands. "We must've won. They wouldn't be coming back together if we didn't."

I rub my arm as I watch their majestic flight. "Surely, they will spot Loki from their height."

Anita shrugs. "Maybe. But they might not recognize him, especially if he shapeshifts into something they haven't seen before or even into a Valkyrie."

"Is that possible?" I realize my stupidity as soon as the words leave my mouth. Of course I know it's possible. He posed as a wingless Valkyrie when I was at the academy. Another sense of dread travels through me as I watch them come in. I hope they'll pick up on him on the way back.

Mistress Sigrun is the first to land not far from Elan. She pulls at her tan leather fighting jacket, snapping it together. "I see you've healed the dragon." Her eyes travel to Anita. "You've done well with this one, healer."

Anita's throat moves awkwardly as she undoubtedly swallows away her nervousness, fighting the urge to tell the mistress the truth. Instead, she inclines her head. "Thank you, mistress." Gratitude fills her voice even though she knows that she's not responsible.

The mistress nods her approval.

"Did you defeat the monster?" Eir asks.

The mistress's chin lifts. "Of course. How could it succeed against all of us and Thor's lightning and hammer? One monster against the majority of Asgard's fighters doesn't have a chance."

I worry my upper lip before blurting, "Did you see any other unusual beings or foreign threats on your way back?"

The mistress chuckles. It's a strange sound from her and something I never heard in my years at the academy. "Like what?"

I toss a hand dismissively. "You know, like frost giants or dark elves?" I try to sound blasé.

The mistress chuckles again. "No. We didn't see any more threats. If you don't mind, I'm going to get cleaned up and ready for class." She disappears into the academy, and my brow pinches into a frown as I watch her vanish into a cloud of winged Valkyrie Academy students. When she's out of earshot, I face my friends and the healer. "What are we going to do? I have to find Loki. If the Valkyries didn't see him, where has he gone?" I groan. "I'm officially wrecked. My life as Thor's respected dragon rider is over."

. . .

THE END

~~~~~

Pursuit: Released October, 2020

FREE SHORT STORY

Fenrir's Journey to Asgard HERE (https://dl.
bookfunnel.com/8glo62ay9e)

ACKNOWLEDGMENTS

Thank you to all of the creators of literature and websites who have spent time writing about Norse Mythology. Even though at times there has been contradicting information, it has been an interesting study. After all, of course a goat produces mead, and a dragon gnaws at the roots of the Yggdrasil, unhindered, threatening the existence of the nine realms attached to the world tree. Plus, there are many other "believable" tales told.

Norse mythology is such an impressive set of tales that I have incorporated some and invented others to create Kara and Elan's story.

I am touched by the enormous amount of support I have received from my immediate family. My husband has been a helpful first reader and, at times, been an excellent motivator, with hints of ideas to help me through the blanks. The support from my three sons has also been overwhelming. They have spent years putting up with my head in the clouds, thinking about the next plot twist or story, along with many hours spent working on my books and keeping in touch with my readers.

A big thank you to my extended family, who support me being a book enthusiast.

A huge thank you to my editor, Amanda K., her editing and writing tips, and my Proofreader, Kristina B, for picking up the things we missed.

Thank you to all of my readers who have loved my work, and continue to read my stories.

BOOKS BY KATRINA COPE

Pre-Teen Books

The Sanctum Series

JAYDEN'S CYBERMOUNTAIN

SCARLET'S ESCAPE

TAYLOR'S PLIGHT

ERIC & THE BLACK AXES

ADRIANNA'S SURGE

~~~~~

Young Adult Urban Fantasy

Afterlife Series

FLEDGLING

THE TAKING

ANGELIC RETRIBUTION

DIVIDED PATHS

TRUTH HUNTER

Afterlife Novelette

THE GATEKEEPER

~~~~~

Young Adult Urban Paranormal Fantasy

Supernatural Evolvement Series

(Associated with the Afterlife Series)

WITCH'S LEGACY (Prequel)

AALIYAH

~~~~~

Young Adult Norse Mythology Fantasy

Valkyrie Academy Dragon Alliance

MARKED

CHOSEN

VANISHED

SCORNED

INFLICTED

EMPOWERED

AMBUSHED

WARNED

ABDUCTED

BESIEGED

DECEIVED

Thor's Dragon Rider

SAFEGUARD

PURSUIT

ENTRAPMENT

Get updates & notifications of giveaways

Would you like a FREE ebook?

Click here to get started: FREE copy of Marked or go to
https://dl.bookfunnel.com/f4cm1zh2qb

Through this link you can sign up for my newsletter and
receive a FREE copy of Marked plus updates about my
fantasy books, sales and notification of giveaways.

ABOUT THE AUTHOR

Katrina is a best-selling author of young adult fantasy and middle grade/tween novels. Her novels incorporate action, heart and an intriguing plot.

She resides in Queensland, Australia. Her three teenage boys and husband for over twenty years treat her like a princess. Unfortunately though, this princess still has to do domestic chores.

From a very young age, she has been a very creative person and has spent many years travelling the world and observing many different personalities and cultures. Her favourite personalities have been the strange ones, yet the ones under the radar also hold a place in her heart.

Katrina's online home is at www.katrinacopebooks.com
You can connect with Katrina on:
Facebook Group

facebook.com / Author.Katrina.Cope

twitter.com / Katrina_R_Cope

instagram.com / katrina_cope_author

pinterest.com / katrinacope56

bookbub.com / profile / katrina-cope